Stories for every Season

**Look out for all of these
enchanting collections by** Enid Blyton

IN PAPERBACK

Animal Stories
Springtime Stories
Summer Adventure Stories
Summer Holiday Stories
Christmas Stories
Christmas Treats
Winter Stories

IN HARDBACK

The Famous Five Treasury
Jolly Good Food
Favourite Enid Blyton Stories
Treasury of Bedtime Stories

Enid Blyton

Stories for every Season

with illustrations by
Becky Cameron

HODDER CHILDREN'S BOOKS
First published in Great Britain in 2019 by Hodder & Stoughton
1 3 5 7 9 10 8 6 4 2

A CIP catalogue record for this book is available from the British Library.

ISBN 978 1 444 95089 2

Printed and bound in China

The paper and board used in this book are made from wood from responsible sources.

Hodder Children's Books
An imprint of Hachette Children's Group
Part of Hodder & Stoughton
Carmelite House
50 Victoria Embankment
London EC4Y 0DZ

An Hachette UK Company
www.hachette.co.uk
www.hachettechildrens.co.uk

CONTENTS

SPRING

SUMMER

AUTUMN

WINTER

SPRING

THE THRUSH AND HIS ANVIL

It was a lovely spring morning. The birds were singing and the sun shone into Jane's room so brightly that she woke up early and jumped out of bed without waiting for her mother to come and call her.

I must go out and see how my plants are getting on, she thought. *We have had so many wet days lately that I have not been out in the garden for quite a long time. I'll go before breakfast, while it is fine.*

She dressed quickly and ran out into the garden. The air

3

smelt warm and moist after the rain.

Jane had a little piece of garden of her own that she looked after with special care, and she hoped to find that her plants had grown quite big. So they had, but – oh dear! – nearly every leaf had a piece bitten off it! Jane was most upset. She ran round the rest of the garden, and found that Daddy's plants were just the same. Lots of his young lettuces were eaten too.

She rushed back to the house and burst into the dining room where her parents and her brother Peter were sitting down to breakfast.

'Daddy,' she cried, 'something is eating all our young plants! Something big too – not just a caterpillar or a grub.'

'It's probably the snails,' said her father. 'After all, they have about fourteen thousand teeth on their tongues, you know. They can do a lot of damage in one night! And there are generally a lot of them about after rain.'

'Gracious, have snails got teeth on their tongues?' said Peter. 'I never knew that. Fourteen thousand teeth – why, their tongues must be like rasps then!'

'They are,' said Father, 'like files. Of course, they are not the kind of teeth you and I have, Peter! But they are very strong, and a snail can eat most of a young plant in a night, using his ribbon tongue.'

'But doesn't he wear it out?' asked Jane.

'Yes, but it is always growing,' said Father.

'Well, what are we to do about our snails?' asked Jane. 'We can't let them eat everything in the garden. There must be dozens of them about.'

'Finish your breakfast,' said her father, 'and then we will go and look at the damage.'

They were soon out in the garden and looking at the plants.

Suddenly Father stopped and pointed to something.

'Look at that!' he said. 'We needn't worry much about your plague of snails. Somebody else knows about them and is dealing with them. See that stone? That is the thrush's anvil – the place he comes to when he has caught a snail and wants to smash its shell.'

The children saw a flint beside the path. Round it were scattered many fragments of broken shell.

'Did the thrush really have the sense to come and use this stone for an anvil?' said Peter, half doubtful.

'Well, come into the summerhouse here and we'll watch,'

5

said Father. 'It's always better to see a thing for yourself than to hear about it second-hand. Come along.'

They sat down in the summerhouse and waited. They didn't have to wait long. Soon a thrush with a speckled breast flew down to the stone.

'He's got a snail in his beak!' whispered Jane.

So he had. Then he began to deal with the snail. He struck it hard on the stone anvil again and again. Tap, tap, tap, tap! Tap, tap, tap, tap!

'I've often heard that noise before and I didn't know what it was!' whispered Peter. 'Now I shall know it's a thrush using his anvil!'

The thrush worked hard. The snail shell was strong and it wouldn't break. The thrush beat it down with all his might. Crack!

'It's broken!' said Jane. 'Now he can get at the soft body inside. He's eating the snail, Daddy.'

'Poor snail!' said Peter. 'But he shouldn't eat our lettuces!'

'Clever thrush!' said their father, getting up. 'Well, I think you can leave him to deal with your snails, don't you?'

GILLIAN AND THE LAMB

Once upon a time Gillian went down to the farm to fetch some eggs all by herself.

'I shall take my doll Betty with me,' she said to her mother. 'She has had a bad cold, and the sunny air will do her good. I shan't be long, Mummy.'

So Gillian tucked her doll up well, put her purse with the egg money under the cover of the pram, and set out down the lane, feeling rather proud to think she was out by herself.

She went over the bridge and peeped at the brown stream

underneath. She saw a great many white daisies in the grass, and some early buttercups. She heard a lark singing so high up in the sky that she couldn't see him at all.

'I hope you are enjoying this nice walk,' she said to Betty, her doll, who was sitting up with her woolly hat on her curly hair.

Soon Gillian came to the farm. There were so many hens running about that she had to be quite careful where she wheeled her doll's pram. They said 'Cluck, cluck!' to her in loud, cheerful voices, and she said 'Cluck cluck!' back. It was easy to talk hen language.

She wheeled her pram up to the farm door. She knocked. Nobody came. She knocked again, a bit harder this time. Still nobody came.

'Oh dear!' said Gillian. 'That means no one is in – and I shall have to go home without the eggs. What a pity!'

So she set off home again. She had just passed the field where the big haystack stood when she saw something moving in the hedge. She stopped to see what it was.

'Oh, it's a tiny baby lamb!' said Gillian in surprise. 'It's escaped from the field. Go back, lamb! If you don't, a car may come along and knock you down.'

But the lamb wouldn't go back. It came limping over to Gillian, and then she saw that it had torn its leg on the barbed wire that ran along the hedges there. She knelt down and looked at the leg.

'When I hurt my leg, I have it bathed and some good stuff put on it,' said Gillian. 'Your mother sheep can't do that – but perhaps she will lick it better if you go back to her. Look – there she is, peeping through the hedge at you!'

Sure enough there was a big mother sheep putting her head through the hole in the hedge, baaing loudly. Gillian picked up the tiny lamb and carried it back to the hole – but it wouldn't go through it! It kept limping back to Gillian.

'Whatever shall I do with you, lamb?' she said. 'I can't leave you here in the lane. And you won't go back to your mother. And there is no one at the farm this morning to look after you.'

She stared at the lamb and the lamb stared back at Gillian, 'Maa-aa-aa!' said the lamb in a small, high voice, and it wriggled its tail like a hazel catkin on the hedge.

'I shall take you home to my own mother,' said Gillian. 'She is kind and will know what to do with you. She will make your leg better.'

'Maa-aa-aa!' said the lamb.

'Come along then,' said Gillian. 'Walk close behind me, lamb.' But the lamb wouldn't. It just stood there in the middle of the lane, maaing and wriggling its tail.

'Well, really, I don't know what to do with you!' said Gilllian. And then an idea came into her head. Of course! She could wheel the lamb in her pram! It was quite small enough to go in.

So she picked up the tiny lamb, and put it gently in the pram beside Betty, the doll. 'I'm afraid you will be a bit squashed, Betty,' said Gillian. 'But I can't help it. Lie down, lamb. I'll cover you up nicely.'

The lamb was surprised to find himself in a pram. He lay quite still. Gillian covered him up. She tucked him in well in case he wriggled loose. 'Maa-aa-aa!' said the lamb, and he sniffed at Betty, the doll.

Gillian wheeled the pram up the lane. She met Mr Logs, the woodman. 'Good morning,' he said. 'And how's your doll today?'

'She's a bit squashed because she's sharing the pram with a lamb,' said Gillian. Mr Logs bent to see – and when he saw the little lamb looking at him, how he laughed!

'That's a funny sight!' he said. 'Well, well, well!'

Then Gillian met Mrs Thimble, who did sewing for lots of people. 'Good morning, Gillian,' she said. 'And how's your doll today?'

'She's a bit squashed because she's sharing the pram with a lamb,' said Gillian. Mrs Thimble bent down to see, and how she laughed when the little lamb said 'Maa-aa-aa!' to her.

'No, *I'm* not your ma-aa-aa!' she said. 'I can hear your ma baaing for you in the field!'

'Oh, there's my mummy!' said Gillian. 'I must go and show her my lamb. Goodbye!'

She wheeled the pram in at the gate of Old Thatch. Her mother was weeding a bed nearby. She called her.

'Mummy! Here's a lamb with a hurt leg! It wouldn't go back into its field – and there's no one at the farm – so I've brought it home for you to mend.'

Her mother stood up in astonishment and looked for the lamb. She didn't think of looking into the pram!

'Where *is* the lamb?' she said.

'Maa-aa-aa!' said the lamb, waving one of its feet over the pram cover. How Gillian's mother laughed! She laughed and she laughed to see the lamb lying in the pram with Betty, the doll.

'Whatever will you do next, Gillian?' she said. She took the lamb out of the pram and looked at its leg.

'Go and get me a basin of water,' she said. So Gillian ran off. Very soon the lamb's leg was washed and some good stuff put on it. It wasn't very bad. It didn't even need a bandage, though Gillian badly wanted to put one on.

Just then the farmer's wife came by the gate, home from

shopping, and she looked in. How surprised she was to see the lamb in the garden of Old Thatch!

Gillian told her all about it, and the farmer's wife laughed when she heard about the lamb being wheeled in the pram.

'Thank you for being so kind as to look after it for me,' she said to Gillian. 'I'll carry it back to the field now, and mend the fence.'

So she did – but always after that, when Gillian went down the lane, the little lamb watched for her and maa-ed to her. It put its tiny head through the hedge, and you may be sure that Gillian always stopped to rub its little black nose!

A LITTLE BIT OF MAGIC

Fanny had been reading a book of fairy tales. My goodness, the magic there was in Fairyland! The way wizards changed people into different things – and the way that spells were worked and magic done – it was wonderful!

'Oh, Mummy!' she said when she had finished the book. 'I wish I could see some magic. But I don't believe there is any nowadays. Things don't change suddenly into something else – there don't seem to be any spells about at all.'

'Well, I can show you something that seems like magic,' said

her mother. 'Something that happens a hundred times every year in everyone's garden.'

'Show me, Mummy!' said Fanny, really excited.

So her mother took her out into the garden. She went to the cabbage patch and hunted about. She turned back a leaf with holes in and showed Fanny a green and yellow caterpillar there.

'We'll take this caterpillar on a piece of leaf, and watch him use a spell to change himself into something else,' she said.

So she and Fanny took the little caterpillar to Fanny's bedroom on a piece of cabbage leaf. Mother found a box and made holes in it. She put a piece of glass over the top so that Fanny could watch the tiny creature eating his cabbage-leaf.

'Has anyone told you what a caterpillar can turn himself into?' asked Fanny's mother. But Fanny was only six, and she didn't know.

'Well, this caterpillar can turn himself into a butterfly with wings,' said Mother.

'However can he do that?' said Fanny in surprise, looking at the long caterpillar. 'I can't see the beginnings of any wings at all.'

'He hasn't got even the beginnings now,' said her mother.

'He gets those later when the magic begins to work. We will watch him each day.'

So they watched the caterpillar. Twice he grew so fat that he had to change his tight skin. Fanny was surprised to find he had a new one underneath each time. She gave the little caterpillar a new cabbage leaf every day and he grew and grew.

One day he didn't want to eat any more. He went into a corner of the box and began to spin a kind of silky web there. Fanny couldn't think where he got it from.

But he had plenty of silk. He fixed himself safely in the corner – and then a strange change came over him. He changed his skin for the last time. He lay still. He became hard and brown. He seemed quite, quite dead.

'He seems just a hard little case,' said Fanny, puzzled. 'He isn't like a caterpillar any more. But he isn't like a butterfly either. His magic must have gone wrong, Mummy.'

'We'll wait and see,' said Mother. 'We call him a chrysalis now. Watch carefully each day.'

Fanny watched – and one day she was very excited. 'Mummy, Mummy! I believe there is a butterfly being made inside the caterpillar's hard brown case! I can faintly see the

outline of wings – and what looks like new legs all bunched up together! Look!'

Her mother looked – and as she looked, a magical thing happened. The case split down the back! It began to move and wriggle – and suddenly out of the split came a small head!

'Something's coming out – something's coming out! Look!' squealed Fanny.

Something did come out – something with four white crumpled wings, six thin legs, and a head with pretty trembly feelers on it! Something so unlike a caterpillar that it was quite impossible to think there had ever been a caterpillar inside the case.

'It's a pretty white butterfly!' said Fanny. 'A butterfly with wings! Mummy, how did it grow wings? It hadn't any when it turned into a chrysalis. How can a caterpillar turn into a butterfly? Do, do tell me.'

'I don't know,' said her mother. 'Nobody knows. It's a little bit of magic. The caterpillar goes to sleep and wakes up as a butterfly. It's like the tale of *Beauty and the Beast* – you remember how the ugly Beast turned into the beautiful prince? Well, that's the same sort of thing that the caterpillar does.'

'It's real magic,' said Fanny, watching the butterfly dry its crumpled wings in the sunshine. 'Soon it will fly away and be happy in the flowers. It won't eat cabbage leaves any more. It's a butterfly!'

Have you watched this bit of magic? You ought to. It's just as strange as anything that happens in Fairyland, isn't it?

CONFETTI AND BELLS

'Pip! Wherever can you be?' called Aunt Twinkle. 'Oh, there you are. Listen, I want your help.'

'What sort of help?' asked Pip the pixie. 'I don't want to sweep or scrub or . . .'

'No, that's not the kind of help I want this time,' said Aunt Twinkle. 'Didn't you know that the sailor doll and Tilly, one of the doll's house dolls, are getting married today?'

'Are they?' said Pip. 'Well, I'll go to the wedding then. But what sort of help do you want, Aunt Twinkle?'

'The toys haven't got any confetti to throw over the sailor doll and Tilly,' said his aunt. 'And they haven't got any bells to ring either. Can you and Jinky manage to get some in time for the wedding?'

'Yes, of course!' said Pip. 'Jinky, come and help. We've got to get confetti and bells for a wedding.'

The two pixies ran off. First they went to the bluebell glade, and picked six fine bluebells. They pulled the blue bells from the stalks and threaded them on silver thread. They put a ringing spell inside, and then went back to hang them up for the toys.

'They'll ring at exactly the right moment,' said Pip. 'Now we're off to get the confetti. We'll be back in a minute!'

They ran to the hawthorn hedge. The may was in full bloom, and its sweet, spicy scent filled the air. Pip looked up at the masses of snow-white blossom.

'Blow, wind, blow for a few minutes!' he cried, and the wind blew. Down fluttered a thousand tiny white petals from the may hedge and fell over the ground.

'Pick them up, Jinky,' said Pip.

The two picked up all the white petals, popped them into paper bags and ran off to the toys.

'The finest, sweetest-smelling confetti in the world!' said Pip. 'Where's the bride? Here she comes!' And he threw handfuls of confetti over her – how pretty the petals looked flying in the air. Then the blue bells began to ring, and everyone cheered.

Who had the biggest slices of the wedding cake? I'll leave you to guess!

HOW VERY SURPRISING!

'I've planted my seeds!' called Sandra. 'And I've put labels in to show what they are.'

Mother came to look at Sandra's little garden. It had one rose tree in it and a pansy plant. The rest of it was bare brown earth, where Sandra had planted her seeds.

'You'll have to water them if the weather stays dry, Sandra,' said Mother.

'But I haven't a watering can,' said Sandra.

'You can borrow Pat's – ask him if you may,' said Mother,

so Sandra went to ask her big brother.

'Can I borrow your watering can, Pat, to water my seeds when they grow?' she asked.

'No, you can't,' said Pat, looking up from his book. 'I lent you my scissors and you lost them. And I lent you my new book and you tore a page. I'm not lending you anything else.'

'I bought you some *new* scissors!' said Sandra. 'And it wasn't my fault the book got torn – I just left it open on the table and the kitten got up and scratched at the page.'

Pat said nothing. He just went on reading. Sandra ran off to find her little basket. She would weed all round the edges of her garden and make it look neat!

Her seeds soon came up. She saw them in little green rows and patches and felt very pleased. The ground looked very dry because there had been no rain, and Sandra wondered if she should water her seedlings.

'Yes, of course,' said Mother.

'But Pat won't lend me his watering can,' said Sandra. 'I asked him.'

'Well, that's rather selfish of him,' said Mother. 'You can't possibly hurt his can – or even lose it!'

'Can I use Daddy's?' asked Sandra.

'No, dear – it's far too heavy,' said Mother. 'Let me see now – what *could* you use?'

'What about the old nursery teapot?' said Sandra. 'The spout's broken off halfway and the lid is broken too – and you said you couldn't get it mended, so it's never used now. Could I take that to water my seedlings with? It would be just about right for them.'

Mother laughed. 'What an idea – to water your garden with a teapot! Yes, I don't see why you shouldn't take it, dear – I shan't use it any more now. Keep it for yourself.'

Sandra was pleased. She ran off to get the teapot with the broken spout. She was glad to use it because she had always loved it. It had rabbits and chicks all over it, and she was sure it was sad because no one ever used it now.

She went down the path to the garden tap and filled the little teapot. Then she carried it to her garden and watered all her green seedlings carefully. The teapot dripped cold water gently over them, and Sandra thought how pleased they must be to have a drink when they were so thirsty.

'I'll leave you here, in the long grass by my garden,' she said, and put the teapot down there. 'Then Pat won't see you and take you away and hide you. He isn't always very kind, you know.'

The teapot settled down in the long grass. Pat didn't see it when he came by. He noticed that Sandra's garden had been watered, and wondered if she had used his can. He went to ask her.

'No, I *didn't* borrow your can,' said Sandra.

'But you've been watering your garden!' said Pat. 'What did you use to water it with then?'

'I shan't tell you!' said Sandra. 'It's something Mother gave me, Pat – something we used to use in the nursery – but it's mine now.'

'If we used to use it in the nursery, then it's partly mine,' said Pat. 'What is it? I might not want you to use it.'

But Sandra wouldn't tell him, and he went off crossly. He didn't guess that it was the little nursery teapot, hidden so cosily in the long grass.

The weather was very wet after that. It rained nearly every day, and Sandra didn't have to water her garden at all, so the teapot was quite forgotten. Sandra's seeds grew and grew, and some of them even put out tiny buds. She was very pleased.

Then the weather became hot and sunny, and Sandra thought she really must water her plants again. Now, where had she put that old teapot without a lid?

'Oh yes – in the long grass beside my garden bed,' she said and hunted for it. 'Ah, here it is, but oh, it's full of something! Who could have put all this mess inside it?'

Just as she was bending down to pick it up a tiny blue and yellow bird flew round her head. *'Pim-imim-imim!'* he said. *'Pim-imim-imim!'*

'What do you want, bluetit?' said Sandra, surprised. 'Oh, you dear little bird, why are you singing at me like that?'

The bluetit suddenly darted down to the teapot – and went in at the little hole where once the lid had been! Sandra stared in astonishment.

'Why, surely you haven't a nest in there?' she cried. 'You have, you have! Oh – in the old *teapot* – and your front door is where the lid went!'

She peered down and there was the little blue and yellow tit sitting right in the teapot, on the 'mess' inside – but it wasn't a mess; it was a nest!

Sandra could hardly believe her eyes. She raced up in the garden, shouting at the top of her voice.

'Mother! The bluetits are nesting in our garden – and guess where!'

'In my nesting box?' shouted Pat hopefully.

'No! It's nowhere near your nesting box!' cried Sandra. 'Mother, come and see!'

So down the garden went Mother, and Pat ran too. Where *were* the bluetits nesting? Pat had hung up a lovely nesting box for them that he had made himself – and now after all they had nested somewhere else!

'Look, Mother – there's the nest!' said Sandra, pointing down to the teapot. 'In the old nursery teapot you gave me for watering my garden. See – the mother bird is sitting right inside! She gets in through the lid hole.'

'Well! How lovely!' said Mother. 'What a peculiar place to choose – but tits always love to nest in holes of any kind. How lucky you are, Sandra!'

'You ought to share the nest with *me*, because the nursery teapot was as much mine as yours,' said Pat, jealous because he had so badly wanted the tits to nest in the box he had made.

'All right,' said Sandra generously. 'You can share it. I don't know how many eggs are in it – but half can be yours. Oh, to think we'll have heaps of tiny bluetit babies!'

The bluetit flew out of the hole in the teapot, and Sandra peeped in. 'One, two, three, four, five, *six* eggs!' she said. 'Three for each of us. When will they hatch, Mother?'

'I don't know,' said Mother. 'Fairly soon, I expect. But don't

disturb the tits too often, Sandra, or you may make them desert the nest.'

'But I'll *have* to water my garden!' said Sandra. 'See how dry it is, Mother. 'Oh, but I *can't* water it now!'

'Why not?' asked Mother.

'Well, because the tits have got my watering can, of course!' said Sandra. 'I was using it for a watering can, don't you remember?'

'Dear me, yes,' said Mother. She looked straight at Pat, and he went red.

'You can use *my* can, Sandra,' he said. 'But I'm not sorry I wouldn't lend it to you before!'

'Now, Pat, don't be unkind, just after Sandra has said you can share the nest,' said Mother.

'I'm not!' said Pat. 'All I mean is, if I *had* lent Sandra my can instead of saying 'No', she wouldn't have used the nursery teapot – and so the tits wouldn't have been able to nest there – and we wouldn't have had any baby bluetits. That's all!'

'Oh, well then, *I'm* glad too that you wouldn't lend me your can!' said Sandra. 'But I'm glad that I can use it *now*, Pat – because the bluetits need the teapot more than my seedlings do!'

The eggs have all hatched now, and the old teapot is full to overflowing with tiny blue and yellow birds. I do wish you could see them!

THE EASTER CHICKENS

Tommy was staying with Auntie Susan and Uncle Ben at the farm for Easter. Mummy and Daddy had gone away for a holiday by themselves, and Tommy was sorry because he did so like Easter at home. There were coloured Easter eggs on the breakfast table to eat them – and chocolate ones too – and perhaps a fluffy yellow chick tied to one egg, or a little rabbit.

I don't expect Auntie Susan or Uncle Ben know what a little boy likes at Easter, thought Tommy. *I don't expect they will buy me any eggs at all. I wish I was at home with Mummy and Daddy!*

Sure enough, when Easter morning came and Tommy ran downstairs to breakfast, there was no coloured egg for him in his eggcup – only just an ordinary brown egg laid by Henny-Penny, the brown hen.

Tommy looked to see if there were any chocolate eggs for him – but there wasn't even a very small one. He felt very sad.

'Sit down and eat your breakfast, Tommy,' said Auntie Susan. 'We must get on because I have a lot of things to do today.' Auntie Susan always had a lot of things to do. So did Uncle Ben. *Perhaps that was why they hadn't remembered his Easter eggs,* Tommy thought. He remembered how he had seen a little yellow chick in the sweet shop yesterday down in the village. It was carrying an egg. He would have liked that very much. He wondered if he should ask Auntie Susan if she would buy it for him, but he decided not to. Mummy had always said that he mustn't ask for things. She said if he was nice enough, people would always buy him things without being asked because they loved him.

I may not have been nice enough, Tommy thought.

So, instead of being sulky and disappointed, he tried to be extra nice to Auntie Susan, and ate his egg without dropping a single bit of the yellow part on the tablecloth.

'Can I go on any errands for you, Auntie Susan?' he asked, when he had finished breakfast.

'I think Uncle Ben wants you to go down to the hencoops with him,' said Auntie. 'I'm coming too.'

So they all three went down to the hencoops. There were four of these, with four brown hens sitting on thirteen eggs each.

And do you know, when they came to the first hencoop, some of the eggs had hatched! Yes – and there were three yellow chicks running about saying 'Cheep-cheep-cheep!' as loudly as they could.

'Oh!' said Tommy, delighted. 'Look at those dear little chicks, Auntie! Do look at them! They are much sweeter than the toy ones I saw in the shop yesterday! And, oh, look – they have got something tied to their backs – whatever are they carrying?'

'Look and see,' said Uncle Ben with a laugh.

So Tommy crouched down and peeped to see what they were carrying. The chicks had gone into the coop with their mother and it was difficult to see one.

At last one of them came out again – and what *do* you suppose it had got on its back? A little chocolate egg! Fancy that!

'It's carrying an egg, just like the little chick at the sweet shop!' cried Tommy. 'Oh, who is the egg for, Auntie Susan?'

'It's for a nice little boy I know, called Tommy,' said Auntie Susan, laughing. 'That chick has an egg from *me*, Tommy – and that one has an egg for you from Uncle Ben – and the third one has an egg from Mummy and Daddy. It came for you yesterday, and we kept it till Easter Day. Then when the chicks hatched out, we thought you would like to have eggs and chicks together – really proper Easter chicks this time!'

'Auntie! Are the yellow chicks for me as well? Oh I am *so* pleased!'

Uncle Ben caught the chicks and took off the chocolate eggs for Tommy. The little boy cuddled the soft cheeping chicks. Their little bodies were so warm. He loved the tiny creatures – and they were his very own!

'Will they grow into hens and lay me eggs?' he asked.

'Oh yes!' said Auntie Susan. 'You shall take them home with you next week when you go – real live Easter chicks, Tommy for your very own!'

'This is the nicest Easter I've ever had,' said Tommy. 'And I thought it wasn't going to be. What *will* Mummy say when I take home my Easter chicks!'

Tommy still has his chicks – but they are growing into brown hens now and will soon lay him eggs – one for his own breakfast each morning, one for his Mummy, and one for his Daddy. Don't you think he is lucky?

THE BLACKBIRDS' SECRET

Did you know that the blackbird family have a secret that they never tell any other bird or any other creature?

Hundreds of years ago the Prince of White Magic wanted to mend his Well of Gold. This was a strange and curious well, which had always been full of pure golden water. Anything that was dipped into this water became as bright and shining as gold, and was beautiful to see. But, because of so many, many years of usage, the well water had become poor and no longer seemed to have the golden power it once used to have.

40

So the prince decided to go to the Land of Sunlight, and buy enough pure golden rays to make his well golden again. He set off, taking with him a special thick sack so that the sunlight would not be able to shine through the sack and so give away his secret. He bought what he wanted, and by his enchantment imprisoned the sunny gold in the sack. He tied it up tightly and set off home again.

But somehow his secret journey to the Land of Sunlight became known, and the Yellow-Eyed Goblins, who lived in the Dark Forest, decided to waylay the prince as he passed through their kingdom and rob him of the sack. Then they would use it for the Dark Forest, and make it light and beautiful.

Now the prince had made himself invisible, but he could not make the sack unseen. Also, much to his dismay, he found that it was not thick enough, after all, to stop the golden rays from shining through. He would very easily be seen in the Dark Forest. What was he to do?

He called a blackbird to him and asked his advice, and the bright-eyed bird thought of a splendid idea at once. He would ask each blackbird in the forest to spare a black feather from his wing and, with the help of the sticky glue that covered the

chestnut buds on the trees, they would stick the dark feathers all over the sack, and so hide the brightness inside.

In a second this was done. The blackbirds dropped their feathers beside the prince and he rubbed each one in chestnut glue. Soon he had entirely covered the sack with the black feathers, and it was impossible to see it in the darkness of the gloomy forest. He passed safely through the kingdom of the Yellow-Eyed Goblins, for not one of those crafty little creatures caught a glimpse of either the prince or his black-feathered sack.

The sunlight gold was emptied into the old well, and at once the water gleamed brightly. Anything dipped into it became a shining orange-gold, beautiful to see. The prince was delighted. He called the kind blackbirds to him and spoke to them.

'You have helped me,' he said, 'and now I will reward you. All birds like to be beautiful in the springtime. You may make your big beaks lovely to see – so when the springtime comes near, blackbirds, fly to this well and dip your beaks into the golden water. Then you will have bright, shining beaks of orange-gold.'

And every year since then the blackbirds have flown in springtime to the secret golden well, and have come back to us with shining golden beaks.

SUMMER

THE GREAT BIG SHELL

'I don't want to go home, I don't want to go home!' said Janie to herself. She was sitting on the warm sand near a little rock pool. She screwed her toes into the soft sand as she looked out over the blue sea.

'It's the colour of forget-me-nots today!' she said. 'And sounds lovely – it goes *shooooosh – shoo – shoooooosh – shooo*. Oh, I don't want to go home!'

Well, nobody wants to go home after a lovely, lovely holiday! Janie had paddled and bathed, and dug castles, and gone shrimping. She had climbed over the rocks, and had found a cave behind. But now she had to go home again.

She had been ill, and Mummy had sent her away to Granny, who lived by the sea. She wanted to see her mother again – but, oh, how she wanted to take the seaside with her!

I've got a present for Mummy – a little box covered with tiny shells, she thought. *But I'd like to take the smell of the sea and the sound of the sea – and the colour of it! That's what Mummy would like!*

It was her very last day. Tomorrow she went home. She rolled over on her front and peered into a little clear rock pool. And there she saw a very surprising sight!

A crab had caught something in its claws. What was it? It wasn't a shrimp. It wasn't a bit of seaweed. It was something blue that wriggled and struggled.

'It's a sea sprite – the tiniest creature ever I saw!' said Janie, excited. 'As small as a fairy – but I've never seen a fairy! Oh, you bad crab, let go of the tiny thing!'

But the crab held on tight, and at last Janie had to be brave enough to put her hand into the water and get hold of the crab. She opened the claw that held the tiny sprite, and set it free. The

crab scuttled away sideways and suddenly sank into the sandy bottom of the pool and disappeared.

The sea sprite swam up to the top of the pool and spoke in such a high little voice that it sounded like the clink-clink-clink of two pebbles rubbed together.

'Thank you! That was brave and kind of you! The crab was buried in the sand and I didn't know he was there. I walked on him and he put up a claw and caught me.'

'Oh! Aren't you tiny?' said Janie in wonder. 'And your frock is as blue as the sea itself – like forget-me-nots.'

'Is there anything you want?' asked the sprite, seating herself on a little stone near Janie. 'If I can give it you, I will.'

'I'm afraid you can't give me what I want,' said Janie. 'I'm going home, leaving the seaside behind me – and I was just wishing I could take the smell and the sound and the colour of the sea back home with me – to give to my mother.'

'Oh, well, that's easy enough,' said the sprite. 'Wait here a minute. I'll just go and get a big shell – a very big one. I'll be back soon.'

She dived into the pool and disappeared round a corner of a rock. She came back again after a while, dragging a shell as big as herself. She pulled it out of the water and sat down on her stone again.

'I've brought you the smell and the sound of the sea,' she said. 'I went to a friend of mine who is very clever. I asked him to put the things you wanted into this big shell, so that you could carry them home to your mother.'

Janie looked at the shell in wonder. 'Do you mean that?' she said. 'Why, it's like magic!'

'Smell the shell inside,' said the sprite.

So Janie picked up the wet shell and smelt inside it. Oh, the smell of the sea, the rich, salty smell she loved! She sniffed and sniffed!

'Lovely!' she said. 'How clever to put the right smell inside. But what about the *sound* of the sea?'

'Put the shell to your ear and listen,' said the tiny creature.

So Janie held it up to her left ear. She listened – and, will you believe it, there *was* the sound of the sea inside the shell. Yes, the smell was there, and the sound too. How wonderful!

'What about the colour?' she asked, her eyes shining in delight.

'That's more difficult,' said the sprite. 'But look – will you

take my blue sash? That's *exactly* the colour of the sea today! You can tuck it into the shell yourself.'

She undid her sash and gave it to Janie. The little girl slipped it into the big shell. It gleamed there as blue as the sea.

'Thank you!' said Janie. 'Mummy will be *so* pleased!'

'See you next year!' said the sprite and slid into the water with hardly a splash.

Janie took the shell home to her mother. It's a beauty. It sits on her mother's mantelpiece as quiet as can be. But pick it up and put it to your ear. *Shooooooooooosh-shooooo! Shooooooooosh-shoo!* You will hear the sound of the sea inside the shell and smell it too. If Janie is there, ask her to show you the colour of the sea, and, if her best doll's house doll isn't wearing it, she will pull the sash from the inside of the shell, and show it to you.

Listen to the next big shell you see. It's sure to have the sound of the sea inside it, just like Janie's!

THE LITTLE FAWN

For days the sun had shone from a cloudless sky, and the oak leaves hung dry and dusty on the tree. The poppies flaunted their red frocks at the fieldside, throwing off their light green caps in the early morning, and flinging down their red petals at night, as if they really were too hot to wear anything at all. Butterflies of all kinds came to the pink and white bramble flowers on the hedgerow, and wasps and bees hummed from dawn to dusk.

The hedgerow was thirsty. The grass beneath was parched

and brown. Everything wanted the cool rain. The pond water fell lower and lower, and the fish began to be anxious. What would happen if they had no water to swim in? The moorhens talked of going to the big river, but they were fond of the little pond and stayed.

And then, late one afternoon, the rain came. Great purple-black clouds sailed up from the south-west and covered all the sky. It seemed very dark after the brilliance of the summer sun. Then suddenly a flash of bright lightning tore the sky in half, and the startled birds flew to the hedge for shelter. Almost at once there came a loud peal of thunder that rolled round the sky, and sent the young rabbits scampering back to their burrows in fright.

And then, what a downpour! First came big drops that made wide round ripples on the pond, and set the oak-tree leaves dancing up and down. Then came a deluge of smaller drops, beating down faster and faster. The old toad crawled out from his stone and lay in the rainstorm, his mouth opening and shutting in delight as he felt the rain trickling down his back. Crowds of young frogs jumped out of the pond and hopped to the ditch for joy. The hedgehog found a sheltered place and

curled up in disgust, for he didn't like the way the rain ran down his prickles. It tickled him.

Soon a delicious smell arose from the field and hedge – the smell of the rain sinking into the earth. All the animals sniffed it. It was good. In their ears sounded the rippling and gurgling, the splashing and the dripping of the rain. They heard every plant drinking greedily. They heard the excited moorhens scuttling in the rain over the pond. It was a glorious time.

The clouds grew blacker. The lightning flashed again and the thunder growled and grumbled like a great bear in the sky – and just as the storm was at its height there came the sound of tiny galloping hooves. They sounded through the pattering of the rain, and all the rabbits heard them and peeped out of their holes, the rain wetting their fine whiskers. The toad heard them too and crawled back to his hole. He did not wish to be trampled on.

The newcomer ran to the hedgerow and stopped there in its shelter. It was a small fawn, a baby deer, only a few weeks old. The hedgerow was surprised, for it had never seen a fawn before.

The little fawn was trembling. Its soft eyes were wide with fright, and its tail swung to and fro. Another peal of thunder

sounded overhead, beginning with a noise like a giant clapping of hands. The fawn closed its eyes in terror and sank down on the grass.

It was frightened of the storm. Its mother had left it safely hidden in the bracken of the distant wood, and had told it to stay there until she returned. But then the storm had come, and the little fawn, who had never seen lightning before, or heard thunder, had been terrified. The jays in the wood had screamed in delight at the rain, and the fawn had thought they were screeching in terror. Fear had filled his small beating heart and he had run from his hiding place, through the wood, across the fields – anywhere, anywhere, to get away from this dreadful noise and terrible flashing light.

But the storm seemed to follow him. The rain came and lashed him, beating into his eyes. The thunder rolled exactly above his head – or so it seemed to him. Where was his mother? Why did she not come to him? He was so frightened that his legs would no longer carry him and he sank down on the grass beside the old hedgerow.

He made a little bleating sound and the old mother rabbit, who had heard many young animals crying for their mother,

looked out of a hole nearby. She saw the frightened fawn and was sorry for him. She ran out of her burrow in the rain and went up to the panting fawn.

'Don't be afraid,' she said. 'It is only a thunderstorm. It will pass. Be glad of the good rain, little creature, and lick it from the grass. It will taste good.'

The fawn looked at the soft-eyed rabbit and was comforted. It was good to see another creature near him – one that was not frightened. He put out his hot tongue and licked the wet grass. The raindrops were cool and sweet. He stopped trembling and lay calmly in the rain.

'Come under the hedgerow,' said the rabbit. 'You will get wet lying there. This hedgerow is thick and will shelter you well till the storm is past.'

The little fawn obediently pushed his way into the hedge and lay down in the dry, though he could easily reach the dripping grass with his pink tongue.

'Where do you come from?' asked the rabbit inquisitively. 'I have never seen you before, though I have heard my mother tell of creatures like you in the woods.'

'I am a young fallow deer,' said the fawn, looking at the

rabbit out of his beautiful big eyes. 'I was born this summer. I live in the wood with my mother, and I have a fine hiding place there among the high bracken.'

'Bracken is good for hiding in,' said the rabbit. 'Where are your antlers, little fawn? I thought deer had antlers on their heads.'

'I have none yet,' said the fawn. 'But next year they will begin to grow. They will look like two horns at first, but in the second year they will grow more like antlers and every year they will grow bigger and bigger, until I am fully grown and have great antlers like those on my father's head.'

'Surely those big antlers are a nuisance to you?' said the rabbit in surprise. 'Don't they catch in the tree branches as you run?'

'No,' said the fawn. 'We throw our heads backwards as we run, and then our antlers lie along our sides and do not catch anything. Also they protect our bodies from any scratches or bruises we might get as we run through the trees and bushes. My mother has no antlers – but I shall grow some soon.'

'Do you wear them all the year round?' asked the rabbit.

'Oh, no,' said the fawn. 'They drop off in the springtime and

then grow again in a few weeks. On my head I have two little bumps, and it is from these I shall grow my antlers each year. My father has wonderful antlers, very large and spreading, and they show what a great age he is. But he will drop his antlers next springtime, and they will have to grow again from the knobs on his forehead. That is what my mother told me.'

'How strange!' said the rabbit, looking at the little dappled fawn as he lay under the hedge. 'What do you eat, little creature?'

'Oh, I eat grass and toadstools and the shoots of young trees,' said the fawn, beginning to feel hungry. 'And often we eat the bark of trees. I should like something to eat now.'

'There are some turnips in the field on the other side of the hedge,' said the rabbit. 'Would you like some?'

The fawn did not know what turnips were, but he jumped to his feet and followed the rabbit, squeezing himself through the hedge. The storm was over now, but the rain still fell gently. The thunder was muttering far away over the hills, but there was no longer any lightning. Blue sky began to appear between the ragged clouds and once the sun peeped through.

All the hedgerow was hung with twinkling raindrops. The oak tree shone brilliantly, for every one of its leaves had been

well washed by the rain. The fawn slipped into the turnip field and began to nibble at the young turnips. They were delicious. When he had eaten enough he went back to the hedgerow. The rabbit followed him and told him that he should go back to the woods, for his mother would be anxious about him – but at that very moment the blackbird in the tree above sent out his alarm cry.

'*Kukka-kuk!* Beware! Here comes a strange enemy!'

Every animal scuttled back to its hole, and all the birds flew to the topmost branches. The little fawn stood up and smelt the air. Suddenly he made a strange welcoming sound and rushed up to the newcomer. It was his mother, a big well-grown deer with soft eyes and small neat feet with cloven hooves.

She nuzzled her fawn in delight. She had missed him from his hiding place and had come to seek him.

'Come,' she said to him. 'You should not have run away, little fawn. Enemies might have seen you and captured you. You are safe under the bracken in the woods.'

'But a loud and flashing enemy came,' said the fawn, rubbing himself against his mother lovingly. 'I was afraid.'

'That was only a storm,' said his mother.

'There are good turnips in the field over there,' said the little fawn. 'I have eaten some.'

'We will stay under this hedge until the dark comes,' said the deer. 'Then we will feast on the turnips before we return to the woods. Let us find a dry place.'

Under the thick ivy was a big dry patch, for the ivy leaves made a dense shelter there. The deer lay down with her fawn beside her and they waited until evening came. They lay so quiet that none of the hedgerow folk feared them, and the little mice, the hedgehog and the toad went about their business just as usual.

After they had fed on the sweet turnips the little fawn called goodbye to the old rabbit who had been so kind, and then in the soft blue evening time the two trotted back to the woodlands.

'Come again!' called the rabbits, who liked the gentle deer. 'Come again and share our turnips!'

POCKETS IN HIS KNEES

'Hey!' cried Binky the elf to a bee flying by. 'Give me a lift, will you?'

'Where to?' said the honeybee, slowing down a little, his strong wings fanning the air and making quite a draught.

'I've got to take these parcels to Old Man Kindly,' said Binky. 'Very important. He wants them for a spell today.'

'What's in the parcels?' said the bee, flying down beside Binky. 'Are they heavy?'

'No, small and light,' said Binky. 'Keep your feelers out of

them now! We mustn't even *look* inside!'

'All right. I'll take you,' said the bee. 'Hop on my back. But for goodness' sake hold tight, because the last time I gave someone a lift – let me see, who was it now? Oh, yes, it was Bobo – he fell off, and as he fell a swallow snapped him up, thinking he was an extra large fly. Dreadful shock for him. He only just got away in time.'

'I'll certainly hold tight,' said Binky, and he climbed on to the bee's brown back. He took his parcels with him, but it was very difficult to hold them and to hold tightly to the bee's back too.

'Wait, wait!' cried Binky in panic, as the bee's wings began to whirr. 'I'm not ready. I can't hold on with both hands because of Old Man Kindly's parcels.'

The bee stopped whirring his wings. 'Put the parcels in a bag and sling the bag over your shoulder,' he said sensibly.

'Haven't got a bag,' said Binky. 'Bother! I've dropped one of the parcels. Now I'll have to get off and pick it up.'

'We shall never be off!' said the bee impatiently. 'Put the parcels in your pockets, Binky.'

'I haven't any pockets either,' said Binky. 'What about you, Bee? Haven't *you* any pockets?'

'Yes. But they are full already,' said the bee.

'Full! What of? And where *are* your pockets?' asked Binky in surprise.

'In my knees,' said the bee. 'Didn't you know that bees have nice little pockets there?'

'No, I didn't,' said Binky, peering over the bee's body to look. 'Yes, I can see them! What a funny place to have pockets! And whatever have you got in them? They're full of yellow stuff.'

'Yes. I've been collecting pollen to take back to the hive, to make pollen bread,' said the bee. 'I stuff it into my knee pockets. I was just going back to the hive when you called me.'

'I say, Bee – I suppose you wouldn't empty your pockets and let me put my parcels in them, would you?' said Binky. 'Then I could have my hands free, and my parcels would be quite safe. I could hold on tightly.'

'All right,' said the bee, and he emptied all the yellow pollen from his pockets. 'Now put your parcels in, but do be quick.'

Binky stuffed his tiny parcels into the bee's pockets, then held on tightly as the bee rose into the air with a loud humming of wings. He flew with him to Old Man Kindly's cottage set in the midst of the moorland. 'Wait for me, and take me back, Bee,' cried Binky, and he disappeared into the cottage.

Old Man Kindly was delighted to see him and the parcels of magic for his new spell. 'This is really very kind of you,' he said. 'Now what will you have as a reward for your kindness, Binky?'

'Well, *I* don't want a reward,' said Binky, 'but you could perhaps reward the bee who brought me and my parcels here, Old Man Kindly. He let me stuff my parcels into his knee pockets, so that I could have both hands free to hold on with.'

Old Man Kindly went out to the waiting bee. 'I hear you have been helpful and kind,' he said. 'Look around you at my moorland. The heather is out and full of honey. Help yourself, bee, and take as much as you like!'

'Heather honey!' buzzed the bee joyfully. 'Best in the world! Thank you very much indeed.'

And off he went to feast and to take back to his hive as much as he could carry. Binky went with him, enjoying licks of honey *and* a lovely ride.

'Thanks for lending me your knee pockets!' he said the bee. 'I never knew you had any before!'

Did *you* know that a bee had pockets in his knees? You didn't? Well, watch the bees coming and going to the flowers in your garden, and you'll soon see how they pack the yellow pollen into their pockets. Isn't it a clever idea?

BUSY-ONE, HELP ME!

A small poppy plant grew by the wayside. It shivered and shook when the cows came down the lane, afraid that they would tread it down and break it. It trembled when the goats came by on their way to the common, because goats will eat anything.

But it was the little grey donkey that really did the damage. He came wandering along and stood looking over the gate into the field, his left hind foot so near the poppy plant that the hairs on its leaves touched the hairs on the donkey's leg.

The donkey moved his hoof and scraped the little plant right out of the ground without even knowing that he had touched anything. He wandered on, and left the plant lying on the ground, its roots out of the earth.

The sun shone down and the plant grew dry and shrivelled. It was almost dead when Busy-One the brownie came by. It called to him feebly.

'Busy-One! Help me!'

Busy-One ran up. He soon saw that the poppy plant was almost dead. 'I'll plant you again,' he said. 'I'll water you. Take heart, poppy, you'll soon be all right!'

He made a hole with his small hands and tucked the roots into it. He patted the earth down on top. Then he fetched a tiny watering can from his shop, and watered the poppy at the roots.

'Oh, what a lovely drink!' said the poppy. 'You've saved my life, Busy-One. Now I shall be able to grow again, and send up my buds.'

'It's a pleasure to help you!' said the brownie. 'Now I must go back to my shop.'

'What do you sell?' said the poppy.

'Anything and everything!' said the brownie. 'Hats, silks and satins, cups and saucers, plates, cruets, clotheslines . . .'

'Oh, well, if you want hats – or silk for party frocks – or the latest style pepperpots, come to *me*!' said the poppy. 'I can give you all those, Busy-One!'

The Brownie laughed. 'Well, I'll come if I want any of those – but you can't give me anything I can sell, poppy!'

Off he went. The poppy's roots drank the water he had given them, and the little plant was soon growing strongly again. It

put up many buds, drooping their little heads on their stalks. The buds wore green hairy caps, and inside, carefully folded, were the delicate red silk petals of the poppy flower.

The buds grew tall on their stems – they lifted up their drooping heads – and the green caps began to loosen.

The poppy called to a little beetle running along at top speed. 'Beetle – go to Busy-One the brownie and tell him I have some fine green caps for him if he can sell them!'

The beetle ran off at top speed to tell Busy-One and soon the brownie came along with a basket. 'What caps do you mean?' he asked the poppy.

'The little green caps that cover my silken flowers!' said the poppy. 'I will throw them down to you. My flowers are ready to come out, and their green caps will drop off!'

Thud! Thud! Down came the prettiest green caps and the brownie picked them up in delight. Why, they were just the thing for the pixies – they would fit their little heads beautifully!

They did, of course – and the pixies paid well for them. Busy-One picked up every green cap that the poppy dropped and sold it.

Then a day came when the poppy sent the beetle to him

again. 'Tell Busy-One that I have some fine red silk for him if he would like to have it for making party frocks for the elves.'

Along came Busy-One again – and the poppy called to the wind to blow hard. It blew – and each of the full-blown poppy-flowers dropped its red silk petals to the ground. Down they fell one by one, and Busy-One picked them up joyfully.

'What beautiful frocks I can make of this silk!' he cried, and hurried away to set to work. How lovely the elves looked in their red silk frocks, red capes and cloaks, when they went to their midnight parties!

And then another message came to the busy brownie, brought by the tiny beetle. 'Busy-One, the poppy says it has plenty of little pepperpots for you!'

'Now what does the poppy mean by that?' wondered Busy-One. 'Pepperpots! Impossible!'

He hurried off, but there were no little pepperpots on the ground.

The poppy called to him. 'Do you see my seedheads, Busy-One – on the stems where once my flowers bloomed?'

Busy-One looked up and saw the hard brown seedheads, small and round, shaking in the wind. 'Yes,' he said, 'but why

do you call them pepperpots?'

'See what happens when the wind blows hard!' cried the poppy. 'The little brown seedcases are full of tiny ripe seeds, and round the edge at the top are many little windows, tiny holes that have opened to let the seeds shake out when the wind blows. Watch!'

The wind blew, the poppyheads shook, and out of the little row of holes came a shower of tiny poppy seeds that fell all around Busy-One!

He laughed. 'Wonderful! I'll cut off your seedheads, poppy, and I will fill them with pepper and sell them for new-fashioned pepperpots – how everyone will love them!'

He climbed up and cut off all the ripe seedheads. 'Shake out any seeds left inside,' said the poppy, 'and then next year they will grow into poppy plants and you can have plenty of green caps, red silk and pepperpots to sell again! Thank you, little brownie – you've been a good friend to me, and I'm glad I can help you!'

The poppy pepperpots are on sale in Busy-One's shop now, and everyone is hurrying to buy one. Shake-shake – and out comes the pepper! How very clever!

Do look for the green caps, the fine silk petals and the quaint little pepperpots this summer. When the poppyheads are ripe, all the little windows open to let out the seeds in the wind. Now who in the world thought of such a remarkable idea?

THE CROSS OLD MAN

Dan and Daisy were staying at the seaside. It was lovely. The sky was blue, the sun was hot and the sea was as blue as the sky.

The twins paddled in the sea and dug in the sand and bathed all day long. They played with the other children and built some very fine sandcastles with lovely big moats.

One afternoon, when the children were building a fort out of the sand, Dan looked down the beach towards the sea to find out whether the tide was coming in. They wanted to finish building the fort before the sea came right up and washed it away.

'Oh, look – the tide is coming in, and it's almost reached right up to the feet of that old man,' said Dan. 'Do you suppose he knows? Look, the man in the deck chair over there, I mean!'

THE CROSS OLD MAN

'Well, he's looking out to sea, so I suppose he can see the tide coming in!' said Daisy. 'And anyway, he's a horrid old man. He's always cross and shouting.'

The tide crept right up to the old man's feet. Dan was surprised that he didn't move. He ran down and had a good look at him.

'He's asleep!' he said to the others. 'I do think we ought to wake him.'

'Well, when my dog barked and woke him up on the beach yesterday he was very cross. He shouted at me and then he threw a stone at my poor dog,' said one of the boys.

'That was very mean of him,' said Daisy. 'No, don't wake him up, Dan. Let him stay there and get wet.'

'No, we can't do that,' said Dan. 'You know what Mother always says – if people do nasty things to you, it is no reason why you should do nasty things to them. I think I am going to wake him up – even if he does shout at me for doing it!'

So Dan went to wake the old man. He touched him gently on the arm.

'Wake up, sir! The tide is coming in.'

The old man woke up.

'Dear me! So it is! What a very kind little boy you are! Thank you!'

And do you know what the old man did? He bought ice creams for every one of the children on the beach who were building the fort! What a lovely surprise that was! He wasn't such a cross old man after all! Dan was so glad he had woken him up.

THE THREE SAILORS

Tom, Joan and Eric were staying by the sea. Their house was almost on the beach. It was lovely. Every day they had tea on the beach, and Granny, Mother and Daddy came too.

Granny didn't like sitting on the sand to have tea, so Daddy had brought down a wooden table from the house for her. Mother had a tablecloth, and Granny sat up at the table and poured out tea and milk for everyone.

After tea the children wanted to go out in a boat.

'No,' said Daddy. 'Not today. I want to finish my book. Besides, the sea is too rough today. You wouldn't like going in a boat.'

'Oh, Daddy, we should, we should!' said Tom. 'We are such good sailors. Can't we go in a boat by ourselves? We could manage it quite all right.'

'Certainly not!' said Daddy. 'It would never do at all.'

So the children had to be good and dig castles in the sand. Granny helped them. She gave them bits of coloured wool too, to put among the seaweed for flowers when they made a garden for the castle.

'Perhaps Daddy will take you in a boat tomorrow,' she said.

The next day the sea was just as rough, but the children ran to ask their daddy to get a boat.

'No, my dears, the sea is still too rough,' Daddy said. 'You might be seasick.'

'Oh, Daddy, we wouldn't be, really and truly!' said Eric. 'We are such good sailors. Do take us! Oh, do get a boat and let us go out in it!'

But Daddy wouldn't. He said they could none of them swim

well enough to go out in a boat on a rough sea.

'I'm sure I could swim all right if I fell out of a boat,' said Joan, sulking. 'Oh, I do want to go.'

Then Daddy got cross and said nobody was to mention boats again till he did. So the three children set to work to dig, though they all looked rather sulky.

It was Granny who thought of a good idea for them. 'Why don't you turn the wooden table upside down and pretend it is a boat?' she said. 'That would be fun. You could tie the tablecloth to Daddy's stick and tie that to one of the table legs – and you would have a mast and sail! Your spades can be oars.'

'Oooh, yes! We'll play pirates!' cried Eric in excitement. 'Come and help, you others.'

So in a trice the table was turned upside down, and Eric began to tie Daddy's stick to a leg for a mast. Then Joan tied the tablecloth to the stick, and the wind flapped it out for a fine sail. Really, it was most exciting!

'Daddy and Granny and I are going for a walk this afternoon till teatime,' said Mother. 'We will bring tea down with us when we come back. Amuse yourselves well and have a nice afternoon, all of you.'

The three children were left on the beach alone. They were pleased. Now they could play pirates and shout all they wanted to. What a fine boat the big wooden table made!

They got the cushions out of the chairs in the house and put them in the upside-down table. They got their spades for oars. The sail flapped merrily in the breeze.

'Yo-ho for a life on the ocean wave!' shouted Tom. 'We'll have some fine adventures!'

They did! They sailed after ships and caught them. They took prisoners. They had a wreck. They did enjoy their game – and at last they were so hot and tired that they didn't want to play any more.

'I'm going to have a rest,' said Tom, flopping down on a cushion in the upside-down table.

'So am I,' said Joan, fanning herself.

'Let's pretend that we are drifting off to a wonderful treasure island!' said Eric. 'Ship your oars, everyone! While we rest, our ship will take us to a wonderful land where we can find hidden treasure.'

They all lay down on the cushions and shut their eyes. The sun shone down. It was lovely and hot. The little breeze cooled

them nicely. In two minutes all three children were fast asleep.

Now the tide was coming in very fast, with the wind behind it. A big wave ran right up the beach and lapped against the table. The children didn't see it. They were fast asleep, of course. Another wave came, and another. Each one ran up to the table. A bigger wave still ran all around it.

Then such a big wave came that it lifted the table up! It was floating! Two more waves ran under the table – and then, whatever do you think? The waves took that upside-down table and floated it gently out to sea.

Eric's feet were in the water but he didn't notice. Joan's hair hung over the side of the table and got wet, but she was fast asleep. Tom's spade floated off by itself.

The sea was pleased with its boat. It bobbed it up and down, up and down – and suddenly a wave splashed right over the table and woke all three children up with a jump!

They sat up in a hurry. How astonished they were to find themselves out at sea on their table! The beach looked a long, long way away!

'Oooh! Our table's a real boat!' said Tom, looking scared.

'The sea has taken it away!' said Joan.

'We wanted to go out in a boat by ourselves and now we have,' said Eric, not liking it at all.

'I feel sick,' said Tom, holding on to the table, for it was bobbing up and down tremendously on the waves.

'So do I,' said Joan.

'I feel frightened,' said Eric, beginning to cry. 'We can't swim enough to save ourselves.'

'I told Daddy I could, but I daren't,' said Joan.

'Oh, what shall we do?' wept Eric. 'I'm afraid, I'm afraid!'

The three poor sailors clung to the bobbing table for all they were worth. The tablecloth sail flapped merrily. The cushions were soaked every time a big wave broke on the table.

'We shall all be drowned!' said Tom, looking very white.

'If only someone would rescue us!' cried Eric, his tears tasting as salty as the sea spray.

'Look! There's Daddy coming down to the beach with the tea things!' said Joan.

'Yell as loudly as you can,' said Tom.

So they yelled, 'Dad-dee, Dad-dee, Dad-dee!'

Their father was looking around the beach in surprise, seeing no children. Then he suddenly heard their voices and

looked out to sea. How astonished he was to see the three sailors on the table!

'Save us, Daddy, save us!' shouted Tom.

Do you know what Daddy did? He began to laugh and laugh!

'So you are three sailors after all!' he shouted. 'How do you like it?'

'Oh, Daddy, save us!' shouted Joan.

'You silly children, jump into the water and wade to the shore with the table!' yelled Daddy.

'Daddy, we shall be drowned!' wept Eric. 'The sea is so deep!'

'Tom! Jump out and wade to shore!' shouted Daddy again. 'Go on – do as I tell you. I'm not going to wet my nice new trousers to come and fetch you in.'

Tom put one leg over the table into the sea. He clung hard to the table leg and let himself go into the water. Splash!

What a surprise for him! Although he was so far out from shore the sea was only up to his knees. It took a long time for the sea to get really deep at their seaside, for the tide flowed in over level sand.

'Oh! We can paddle back,' said Tom in surprise. 'I'm only up to my knees. Get out, Joan, and help.'

Joan jumped out. Then Eric jumped too – and together the three sailors paddled back to the beach, dragging their table behind them.

'Well, well, well!' said Daddy, still laughing. 'Who's going to worry me to take them out in a boat on a rough sea again?'

Nobody said a word. Nobody wanted to go out in a boat on the rough sea now. The three sailors were rather ashamed of themselves.

But Granny and Mother were quite excited to hear about the adventures, so they all cheered up, put the table the right way up for Granny, and had a lovely tea.

Weren't they funny? I would have loved to see them sailing away fast asleep on their upside-down table, wouldn't you?

THE BOY WHO WOULDN'T BATHE

Once upon a time there was a boy who went to the seaside with his mother and father and sisters and brothers. His name was Thomas, and he had two brothers called Jim and Peter and two sisters called Mary and Emma.

Their mother bought them a bathing suit each, and their father said he would take them into the sea to bathe every morning. So, when the right time came, Thomas, Jim, Peter, Emma and Mary put on their bathing suits and ran down to the water. They had paddled that morning, and loved it – but as

soon as they got out into the sea above their knees, the water seemed to feel rather cold.

'Ooh! It's too cold to bathe!' said Thomas, shivering. 'I'm not going to!'

'Come along!' called his father. 'Wade out to your waist, then dip under! It's fine once you're in.'

Jim waded out and dipped under. So did Emma. Peter took a little longer, but under he went at last – and Mary lost her footing and went under without meaning to! So now they were all wet except Thomas.

And will you believe it, Thomas was still only up to his knees in the water! 'I don't like it; it's cold!' he wailed. 'I'm afraid of the deep sea!'

'Very well,' said his father. 'Stay where you are. You are behaving like a baby, so you'd better stay where the babies stay – at the edge of the water!'

So Thomas stayed at the edge of the water. He thought he would fetch his boat and sail her – so he did. It was a fine boat – not one of those annoying ones that flop over on to their side and lie there – but a proper one with big white sails. It sailed upright, bobbing up and down beautifully.

Thomas held it by a string.

And then the strong wind blew the string out of his hand! His boat floated away from him, away, away on the wind, out to sea!

'Oh, my boat, my boat!' wailed Thomas. But none of the others heard him, for they were all splashing and shouting. Nobody saw the lovely boat sailing away either.

'Come back, boat!' shouted Thomas. But the boat took no notice. It sailed on, right away from Thomas, out towards the deep, deep sea.

Thomas waded after it, crying tears all down his freckled nose. He couldn't bear to lose his beautiful boat. The boat sailed on. Thomas waded out further. He was up to his waist! Did he feel the cold water? No – not a bit! He waded on and on – the sea was up to his shoulders, then up to his chin – and he *just* managed to reach that runaway boat and hold it firmly! A big wave came and Thomas jumped up as it passed him. A little salt water went into his mouth, but he didn't care! He had his precious boat!

'Daddy! Daddy! Look at Thomas! He's out deeper than any of us!' shouted Jim. 'He's braver than any of us!'

His father looked – and he *was* really astonished.

'You're too deep, Thomas!' he shouted. 'Go back! I thought you said you were not going to bathe!'

'I'm not bathing!' shouted back Thomas. 'I only waded after my boat!'

How all the others laughed! Funny old Thomas – wouldn't go out into the water with his brothers and sisters, but didn't think twice about going up to his chin for his boat!

'Your boat has taught you to bathe!' laughed Mary. And so it had – for Thomas wasn't a baby any more after that! He went in the sea every day.

AUTUMN

A BASKET OF ACORNS

The oak tree shook its leaves in the sunshine. The wind blew and the branches waved about. Some of the ripe acorns dropped to the ground below – bump-bump-bump!

A little squirrel came frisking over the ground and saw them. 'Acorns! Nice nutty acorns!' he chattered in delight. 'Plenty for me to eat, and plenty for me to hide away!'

A little dormouse heard the squirrel, and came running out of his nest in the branches.

'Go away!' he squeaked angrily. 'These are my acorns! This

is my tree!'

'Why is it your tree?' said the squirrel in surprise. 'It doesn't belong to you.'

'It does; it does!' squeaked the dormouse. 'I live in it and so it is mine.'

'Well, I often live in the branches, and once I had my nest here, so it is mine too!' chattered the squirrel. He gathered up some acorns in his little paws, and the dormouse ran at him in a rage.

They made such a noise that a big jay came flying down. He screeched loudly and made both the squirrel and the dormouse jump. 'Don't screech like that,' said the squirrel in fright. 'I've told you before, Jay, that you have a dreadful voice.'

'I shall screech as much as I want to,' said the jay. 'Ha! Acorns! So that's what you were quarrelling about! Good! I like acorns! I didn't know there were any ripe yet.'

'These are my acorns!' said the squirrel.

'No, mine, I tell you!' squealed the dormouse.

'Well, they are mine too,' said the jay. 'This oak tree is mine. I have sat in its cool green shade for three years. It is my tree, and it grows its acorns for me and not for you!'

Then what a noise the three of them made, quarrelling about

the fallen acorns. The squirrel no sooner picked up an acorn than the jay pecked it out of his paw – and when it rolled on the ground the little dormouse darted on it and held it! The squirrel made little barking noises, the dormouse squeaked, and the jay screeched at the top of his voice for all the world as if someone were hurting him dreadfully! But he always sounded like that. He really had a very harsh voice!

Three children came along through the trees, carrying a basket. They heard the noise of the jay, the dormouse and the squirrel, and they wondered what the matter was. They hurried up to see.

'Oh, look!' said Amy. 'There is a squirrel – and it is quarrelling with a dormouse and a jay. I wonder why!'

'Let's look and see!' said Ann. 'Come on, you two!'

They ran up to the tree. The squirrel at once bounded up the trunk and disappeared among the leaves. The jay flew off. The dormouse ran into his nest in the tree.

'They've gone!' said Amy. 'Oh, look – this is what they are quarrelling about – acorns!'

She held one up. 'Isn't it pretty? Shall we gather a basketful to take home to Grunter the pig? He will be so pleased to have them. He does like acorns.'

'Yes, do let's take some home,' said the others. So they gathered up a big basketful of acorns.

It was fun to hunt for them in the mossy ground beneath the spreading branches of the great oak tree. The wind in the leaves said 'Sh-sh-sh!' all the time, as if it were whispering a secret.

'Now let's play hide-and-seek,' said Amy. She hid behind the tree, and the trunk was quite big enough to hide her. When Johnnie came round to find her she slipped to the other side, like a squirrel!

When the children had gone home, the squirrel, the dormouse and the jay went to the ground again to hunt for acorns – but not one could they find! The children had taken them all!

'What a pity!' sighed the squirrel. 'We need not have quarrelled – there were plenty of nuts for us all. Now we have none. It serves us right!'

'Sh-sh-sh!' said the oak tree. 'I will send some acorns down for you all tomorrow, if you promise not to quarrel! I have plenty more getting ripe!'

So they promised – and tomorrow they will all eat together like friends. I would like to see them, wouldn't you?

THE TALE OF SNIPS

Snips was a tailor. He made red and yellow coats, brown tunics and cobweb cloaks for party wear. In the autumn he did a roaring trade, for then there were many bright leaves tumbling down from the trees for him to cut up and make into elfin clothes. He was always very busy then.

One year the king himself ordered twelve coats from Snips, all different colours, and each with a hat made of an acorn cup to match. It was a busy time for Snips.

He managed to get them all done, and one night he set out

with the twelve coats in a big bag. With him he took needle and thread, two thimbles and an extra large packet of pins, besides his best silver scissors. Then, if there were any alterations needed, he could do them at once, without taking the coats back again.

The king was delighted with the coats. Not one of them needed to be altered; they all fitted perfectly.

'You're a fine tailor, Snips,' said the king to the proud little goblin. 'I will pay you tonight. You shall have a piece of gold for each coat. Here you are – twelve golden pounds. Take care of them.'

Snips put them into his leather purse, thanked the king and went on his way home, planning all the marvellous things he would do with his money. But there was someone following him – a small green gnome who meant to rob him before he reached home!

Snips didn't know. He went humming along, until he came to the big friendly chestnut tree that stood in the middle of the wood. And just as he passed under it, the leaves began to whisper to him.

'Snips, Snips, there's a robber behind you! Hide, Snips, hide!'

Snips was frightened almost out of his life. He jumped high

into the air, caught hold of a low branch and pulled himself up on it. He sat there trembling. Soon he saw the green gnome passing silently underneath, never guessing that Snips was hidden above him.

'Let me stay hidden in your leaves for the night,' begged Snips. 'In the morning light I can go home safely with my money.'

So he stayed there in safety all the night long. In the morning he asked the chestnut tree what he could do in return for its help.

'I suppose you couldn't stop the horses and donkeys eating my chestnuts when they fall to the ground, could you?' asked the tree. 'It's such a nuisance.'

Snips picked from the tree a round, smooth case, inside which lay two brown, polished chestnuts. 'Of course I can help you!' he cried. 'I'll stick heaps of pins into the cases, head downwards, with their points outwards. Then no animal will like to eat them.'

And that is just what he did. The next year the pins grew from the chestnut cases, and ever since then they have been as prickly as can be. Feel them and see!

HOT POTATOES

'You two go and help Daddy today,' said Mother. 'He's got such a lot to do sweeping up all the leaves. Take brooms and help him.'

'Sweeping is very hard work,' said Sam.

'Well, of course, if you are afraid of hard work . . .' began his mother, but Sam stopped her.

'No, Mother, we're not, really we're not! We'll go and help, and we'll sweep hard,' he said.

The two of them went out. Their father found some small

brooms for them. 'You two are mighty good at playing,' he said. 'Now you let me see how good you are at working.'

The twins began to sweep hard. There were such a lot of leaves! The wind was annoying because it would keep blowing them away.

Father made a bonfire of old twigs, plants and rubbish. 'Do you want to burn the leaves too?' asked Sam.

'No,' said his father. 'They go on the compost heap over there. Susie, you go and ask Mummy for some nice small potatoes, will you?'

'What for?' said Susie.

'Well, sweeping up is hungry work,' said her father, 'and I think we'd all like hot roast potatoes to help us along. Bring me six.'

Susie fetched him six. The twins watched him put them in the hot ashes of the bonfire. 'Will they cook?' asked Susie. 'Will they be nice?'

'Delicious!' said her father. 'Now come along, get to work again.'

How hard they all worked! By the time four o'clock came they were all very hungry indeed. 'I think I'll go and ask Mother

for a biscuit,' said Sam. But his father called him back.

'No, no. If you're hungry, you can have roast potatoes. There are two for each of us. They'll be done now.'

And so they were! Father took them out of the ashes, warm and soft. He and the children ate them standing by the bonfire – and how delicious they were!

'A little reward for hard work!' said Father. 'Hot potatoes for all of us!'

THE LOVELY PRESENT

The little Princess Peronel had been ill. The king and queen were glad when she began to get better, and they hoped very much she would soon be happy and bright again. It was dreadful to see her looking so sad.

In the middle of the month the princess had her birthday, and the king meant to make it a very grand affair.

Perhaps the princess will cheer up when she sees all her presents arriving, he thought. *I will send out a notice to say that everyone must try to think of something really good this year.*

As soon as the people knew that the king hoped for plenty of amusing presents for Peronel, they set to work to make them, for they all loved the little girl. One carved a big wooden bear for her that could open its mouth and growl. One made a whistle from an elder twig that could sing like a bird. There were all sorts of lovely presents!

There was one small boy who badly wanted to give the princess something, but he couldn't think what. He had no money. He couldn't carve a toy. He couldn't even make a whistle. He really didn't know what to do.

Then one day he did a very strange thing. It was a windy morning and the last leaves were blowing down from the trees. The little boy went out with a small sack. He stood under the trees, and every time the wind blew down a gust of dry leaves he tried to catch one. All that day he worked and all the next. In fact, he worked for nine days without stopping, and by that time his sack was quite full!

Then, on the birthday morning, he set out to the palace with the sack of leaves on his back. Everyone wondered what he had! Hundreds of other people were on their way, too, all with toys and presents. But alas for the king's hopes! Not one of the presents made the sad little princess even smile.

Towards the last of all came the small boy with his sack. 'What have you got there?' asked the king in surprise. 'A year of happy days for the little princess!' said the boy. He opened his sack and emptied all the dry, rustling leaves over the surprised princess. Everyone stared in astonishment.

'Don't you know that for every leaf you catch in autumn before it touches the ground you will have a happy day next year?' said the little boy to the princess. 'Well, I have caught three hundred and sixty-five for you, so that's a whole year. They're for you, because I'd like you to be happy and well again – so here they all are! And, as this is the first day of your new birthday year, you must smile and be happy!'

And she did, because she was so pleased.

BLACKBERRY PIE

Andrew was cross. Just as he had planned to go blackberrying with the other children, Mother had called him to go on an errand for her!

'Oh, Mother, I wanted to go and pick some blackberries with Peter and Charlotte!' he grumbled. 'I did want you to make me a blackberry pie tomorrow! It's too bad!'

'I'm sorry, Andrew, but I promised Mrs Jones she should have these books back today,' said Mother, putting four books into a basket for Andrew to carry. 'Now don't sulk – you'll

grow up ugly if you do!'

Andrew said no more. He was fond of his mother, and he wasn't really a sulky boy. So he smiled at her and ran off – but inside he was very disappointed. It would have been so lovely to go blackberrying. There wouldn't be another chance till the next Saturday now, and it might be wet then. Bother, bother, bother!

He met Peter and Charlotte with their little baskets. 'Aren't you coming?' they shouted.

'I can't,' said Andrew. 'I've got to go into the town to take these books to Mrs Jones.'

'Bad luck,' said Peter, and he and Charlotte went on their way to the fields. Andrew began to whistle. He always found that it was a very good thing to do when he felt cross. You can't feel cross if you are whistling!

He came to Mrs Jones's house. She was at home and very glad to have the books. 'It's nice of you to bring them, Andrew,' she said. 'You might have been out in the fields with the others today, and then I wouldn't have got my books!'

'Well, I *was* going blackberrying, but Mother just called me before I went,' said Andrew.

'So you couldn't go blackberrying?' said Mrs Jones. 'What a

pity! But listen, Andrew – at the bottom of my garden a great bramble grows over the fence. I don't like blackberries, so I haven't even looked to see if there are any growing there this year. Would you like to go and see? If there are any you can pick them all!'

'Oh, thank you!' said Andrew, pleased. He went down the garden and came to the bottom – and, sure enough, all over the fence there grew an enormous bramble! And on it were hundreds and hundreds of the biggest, ripest blackberries that Andrew had ever seen! Not one had been picked, and they grew there in the sunshine, full of ripe sweetness.

'Goodness gracious!' said Andrew, astonished and delighted. 'Look at those! My goodness, I'm lucky!' He began to pick them. He ate a great many. They were the sweetest he had ever tasted! More and more he picked, and more and more. His basket began to get full. His hands were wet and sticky. His mouth was purple. He was very happy indeed!

When his basket was full he went to show it to Mrs Jones. 'Splendid!' she said. 'I'm so glad they will not be wasted. Ask your mother to make you a blackberry pie with them. You deserve them.'

On his way home Andrew met Peter and Charlotte, and they were surprised to see his lovely big basketful. They had hardly any, for other children had been to the fields that day and picked all the ripe berries.

'Well, have some of mine!' said Andrew, and he emptied some into their baskets. They *were* pleased! Then home he went – and his mother cried out in astonishment.

'You *have* been blackberrying after all!' How she smiled when she heard Andrew's story – and now a big blackberry tart is baking in her oven. I'd love to have a slice, wouldn't you?

THE LITTLE TOY MAKER

George and Fanny were excited because their mother had said they might go out for a picnic by themselves. 'If you cross over the road very carefully and go to the hill above the Long Field, you should be all right,' she said.

So they set off, with George carrying the picnic basket. In the basket were some egg sandwiches, two rosy apples, a small bar of chocolate, and two pieces of ginger cake. There was a bottle of lemonade as well, and George and Fanny kept thinking of the cool lemonade as they crossed the road, went through the

Long Field and up the hill. They did feel so very thirsty.

There were ash and sycamore trees up on the hill. Already they were throwing down their seeds on the wind – ash spinners that spun in the breeze, and sycamore keys that twirled down to the ground. George picked some up and looked at them.

'Aren't they nice?' he said. 'Throw some up into the air,

Fanny, and see them spin to the ground. The tree is pleased to see them twirling in the wind, because then it knows that its seeds are travelling far away to grow into big new trees.'

After a while the children sat down to have their lunch. They began with the egg sandwiches, but before they had taken more than a few bites they saw a most surprising sight. A very small man, not much taller than George's teddy bear at home, came walking out from behind a gorse bush. He carried two baskets with him. One was empty and one was full. The full one had sandwiches and milk in it, and the children thought that the small man must be having a picnic, as they were.

The little man didn't see them. He had a very long white beard that he had tied neatly round his waist to keep out of the way of his feet. He wore enormous glasses on his big nose, and he had funny pointed ears and a hat that had tiny bells on. The bells tinkled as he walked. Fanny wished and wished that she had a hat like that.

'What a very little man!' said Fanny. 'Do you suppose he is a pixie or a brownie?'

'Shh!' said George. 'Don't talk. Let's watch.'

So they watched. The little man walked along humming

a song – and suddenly he tripped over a root and down he went! His full basket tipped up, and out fell his sandwiches and milk. The bottle broke. The sandwiches split open and fell into bits on the grass.

'Oh! What a pity!' cried George, and ran to help at once. The little man was surprised to see him. George picked him up, brushed the grass off his clothes, and looked sadly at the milk and sandwiches.

'Your picnic is no use,' he said. 'Come and share ours. Do!'

The small man smiled and his face lit up at once. He picked up his baskets and went to where the children had spread their picnic food. Soon he was sitting down chatting to them, sharing their sandwiches, cake and chocolate. He was very pleased.

'Why was one of your baskets empty?' asked Fanny. 'What were you going to put into it?'

'Ash and sycamore keys,' said the small man. 'There are plenty on this hill.'

'Shall we help you to fill your basket?' said George. 'We've eaten everything now and Fanny and I would like to help you.'

'Oh, do,' said the small man. So the three of them picked up the ash and sycamore keys, and put them neatly into the basket.

'Why do you collect these?' asked Fanny. 'I would so like to know. Do you burn them or something?'

'Oh, no. I'm a toy maker and I use them for keys for my clockwork toys,' said the little man. 'Come along home with me, if you like. I'll show you what I do.'

He took them over the top of the hill and there, under a mossy curtain, was a tiny green door set in the side of the hill. The little man pushed a sycamore key into the door and unlocked it. Inside was a tiny room set with small furniture and a big worktable.

And on the table were all kinds of toys! They were made out of hazelnut shells, acorns, chestnuts, pine cones and all sorts of things! The small man had cleverly made bodies and heads and legs and wings, and there were the toys, very small, but very quaint and beautiful. The children stared at them in delight.

'Now, you see,' said the little man, emptying out his basket of keys on to his worktable, 'all I need to do is to find keys to fit these toys, and then they can be wound up and they will walk and run and dance. Just fit a few keys into the holes and see if you can wind up any of the toys.'

In great excitement the two children fitted ash and sycamore

keys into the toys, and George found one that fitted a pine-cone bird perfectly. He wound it up – and the bird danced and hopped, pecked and even flapped its funny wings. It was lovely to watch.

Soon all the funny little toys were dancing about on the table, and the children clapped their hands in joy. It was the funniest sight they had ever seen! They only had to fit a key to any of the toys, wind it up – and lo and behold, that toy came to life!

'I wish we hadn't got to go, but we must. Mother will be worried if we're late,' said George at last. 'Goodbye, little fellow. I do love your toys.'

'Choose one each,' said the little man generously. So they did. Fanny chose the bird and George chose a hedgehog made very cleverly out of a prickly chestnut case and a piece of beechnut. It ran just like a real hedgehog when George wound it up.

And now those two little toys are on their mantelpiece at home, and they are so funny to watch when George and Fanny wind them up with ash or sycamore keys. I can't show you the toys – but you can go and find ash and sycamore keys for yourself if you like. There are plenty under the trees, spinning in the wind. Find a few, and see what good little keys they make for winding up fairy toys!

GRANDPA'S CONKER TREE

'Let's go and see Grandpa today, and ask him if his conker tree has thrown down the rest of its conkers for us,' said Peter to Jean.

So off they went. Grandpa always saw a great deal of the children in the autumn, because they did so like picking up the satiny brown conkers that fell from his chestnut tree.

'Aren't they lovely, Grandpa?' said Jean. 'And I do like their prickly cases. Grandpa, why does the conker tree put its conkers into such prickly green cases?'

'Well, my dear, it doesn't want its precious brown conkers eaten, that's why,' said Grandpa. 'Prickles always stop birds or animals from eating anything. But as soon as the conker is ripe, and ready to root itself and grow, then down comes the case, it splits into three, and out rolls the conker.'

'Grandpa, why did you plant your conker tree in a funny place?' asked Peter. 'It's growing so near the wall of this shed that its branches touch it all the way up to the top.'

'Well, you see – I didn't know I had planted it!' said Grandpa.

'What do you mean?' asked Jean, puzzled.

'I'll tell you about it,' said Grandpa. 'You know, I used to play conkers when I was a boy, just like you do. I used to choose a fine big conker that I thought would be the conqueror of every other boy's chestnut – and we used to hang them on strings, and hold them out for one another to hit in turn.'

'Yes, we like doing that,' said Peter. 'I've got a conker from your tree that is a forty-fiver, Grandpa! It has smashed forty-five other conkers belonging to the boys at my school.'

'Well,' said Grandpa, 'I once had a wonderful conker, fat and solid and strong. I put a string through it, and then I set out to make it conquer every other boys' conker.'

'And did it?'

'It became a one hundred-and-sixer!' said Grandpa. 'What do you think of that? And then one day I was striking another boy's conker, and my hundred-and-sixer flew off the string, shot high in the air – and disappeared!'

'Didn't you find it again?' asked Jean.

'Yes, but not until the spring!' said Grandpa. 'Then I found that my hundred-and-sixer had fallen just behind the shed there – and had lain in the wet grass, put out roots and a shoot – and grown into a beautiful little chestnut tree!'

'Oh, do conkers really grow into chestnut trees?' said Peter, surprised. 'Grandpa, suppose I planted my forty-fiver?'

'Try it and see!' said Grandpa. 'Maybe you will get a big chestnut tree that will throw down conkers for your grandchildren, as mine does for me! That would be fun.'

So Peter is going to plant his conker and see what happens. Have you got one you can plant as well?

WINTER

THE SHIVERY SNOWMAN

One cold winter's day, when the snow was very thick on the ground, two children ran into the fields by Pixie Hill.

'Let's build a snowman!' they cried. 'It would be such fun! There is plenty of snow.'

So they built a snowman – not very large, because they really hadn't much time. He had a nice round head, a short thick body, two arms and no legs at all, but just big feet sticking out at the bottom. They put a pair of old raggedy gloves on his hands, and on his head a dirty old hat, which they found in a nearby hedge. They gave him stones down his front for buttons – and two black stones for eyes. His nose was a bent twig and so was his mouth.

Really, he looked very fine when they had finished with him – quite real, in fact! The children were delighted and they danced round him, shouting loudly.

'We've made a man of snow, of snow, hie-diddle-hie, hie-diddle-o, we've made a man of snow, of snow!'

Then the boy looked at his watch and found that it was almost dinnertime, so off scurried the two children over the snowy fields, back to their home.

The snowman was left alone. A robin flew down and perched on his hat. '*Trilla, trilla,*' he said to the snowman. 'How do you feel, Mr Snowman, out here in the snowy field. Are you lonely?'

The snowman made a little shivery sound. He wasn't quite sure where his voice grew, but he found it at last.

'No, I'm not lonely,' he said. 'I haven't had time to be yet.'

'Wait till it gets dark, and the birds are gone to bed,' sang the robin. 'You may be lonely then. I will tell the little folk who live in Pixie Hill to come and talk to you if you like.

132

You may be frightened in the dark.'

The snowman looked all around him with his black stone eyes. It seemed a very nice world to him. He enjoyed himself very much that day, but when the afternoon changed to evening, he didn't like it at all. He could see nothing then, and he couldn't understand it. He began to feel very frightened indeed.

Suddenly a little voice spoke near to him, and he saw a tiny lantern.

'Good evening, snowman,' said the voice. 'The robin told us about you. We have come to keep you company. Are you lonely?'

The snowman blinked in the light of the lantern. He saw a small pixie holding it – and behind him were about twelve others, all dressed in fleecy overcoats, with pointed fur caps on their heads.

'Good evening,' said the snowman, trying to smile with his bent twig mouth. 'Yes, I was feeling a bit lonely, and a bit frightened too, you know. It is very pleasant to see you.'

The pixies sat down in a ring and looked at the snowman kindly. They were good-hearted little creatures, always ready to do anyone a good turn. One of them put out his hand and touched the snowman. Then he gave a scream.

'Ooooh! How cold you are! Poor, poor thing! If I felt as cold as you, I should cry and cry!'

All the pixies felt the snowman in turn and shrieked in horror to feel how cold he was. The snowman began to feel that he must indeed be cold, and he shivered from head to foot. The pixies saw him and all began talking at once.

'What can we do for him?' Poor, poor creature! Here he is out in the cold open field, with a frosty wind blowing, and not even an overcoat on!'

'We could build a little fence round him of twigs,' said one pixie, running to the hedge at once.

'And I have an old hot-water bottle at home I could lend him,' said another, running to Pixie Hill in a trice.

'And I could bake him two hot potatoes to eat!' said a third, and ran off too.

The others sat and looked at the snowman who was now shivering so much that his hat went all crooked.

'We will make him a nice little fire to warm himself by,' said the other pixies out of the kindness of their hearts. So they set to work to collect dry leaves and sticks and by the time the other three pixies had come back with the little hot-water bottle, and the two hot potatoes, they had made a fine crackling fire, round which they all crowded – for it was certainly a very cold night indeed!

Two other pixies had built a splendid fence round the snowman, and the wind did not feel nearly so cold to his back. He was most grateful. It was lovely to be fussed over like this!

Just then a big white shape swooped out of the night and the pixies screamed in fright. But it was only the barn owl come to see what all the noise was about. When he saw the snowman and the pixies with their fire and fence and all the rest, he hooted and screeched with laughter.

'What's the matter?' cried the pixies crossly.

'Matter enough!' said the old owl with another screech. 'There's such a thing as being too kind, you know! That snowman will be sorry for himself in the morning! Too much kindness is simply foolishness!'

With another loud screech he flew off into the night, leaving the pixies talking angrily about him to one another.

'Nasty old thing!' said one. 'Trying to make out that we are too kind! How can kindness ever be foolish!'

'Don't listen to him,' said the snowman, who was enjoying

all the fussing and petting very much indeed. 'Where is that hot-water bottle, pixie?'

What a time he had! One pixie popped the hot potatoes into his mouth and he swallowed them down. Another gave him the hot-water bottle to hug to his middle with both his gloved hands – and all the rest heaped up the fire and made him as warm as possible.

He suddenly began to feel very sleepy. There was a funny feeling in his middle too, where he was holding the nice hot-water bottle. He thought he really must nod off and go to sleep just for a few minutes.

The pixies went on talking to him. When he didn't answer they were surprised.

'Poor thing, he's gone to sleep!' said one, holding up his lantern, and seeing that the snowman's head had slid a little forward. 'Don't let's disturb him with our chatter. Let's heap up the fire and creep away quietly. He will sleep soundly all night, and wake up well and happy tomorrow.'

So all the pixies crept away, taking their small lanterns with them, and leaving the fire crackling away at the snowman's feet.

The snowman tried to wake up – but he couldn't. He really

felt very funny indeed – much too hot, in fact! The barn owl came sweeping by again, on his great silent wings, and let out a screech of laughter when he saw the old snowman standing all humped up – looking really much smaller now. But the snowman didn't even wake up when the owl screeched.

The night passed. The winter sun rose red in the sky. The pixies came running out to say good morning to the snowman – but where, oh, where had he gone?

He wasn't there! He simply wasn't there! Only the little twig fence stood where they had built it – and some black ashes lay where the fire had been. Hidden in the snow beneath was the hot-water bottle, but the pixies didn't know it had fallen there. They were very much upset.

'He's walked off!' they cried in dismay. 'Oh, how horrid of him! He's taken out hot-water bottle, too! Would you believe it – after all our kindness! He's quite, quite gone!'

They kicked down the little fence they had made, and stamped on the ashes. They were very angry indeed.

'Listen!' said one pixie suddenly. 'I can hear children coming! Quick! Run!'

They scampered off – and soon up came the two children

who had made the snowman the day before. They had brought spades with them this time, and meant to build an even bigger snowman.

'Where's our snowman that we built yesterday?' cried the boy in astonishment.

'He's disappeared!' said the girl, looking all about the field. 'I know quite well this is where we made him yesterday, John.'

'But how can he have disappeared?' wondered the boy. 'It's been very cold and frosty – he ought still to be here. Whatever has happened to him? I do so wish we knew!'

They would have known if they had heard the old barn owl that night screeching to the pixies!

'What did I tell you?' he shouted. 'Didn't I say that too much kindness was foolishness? Well, so it is! You melted that poor wretched snowman till he quite disappeared! He didn't walk away – he melted down to nothing! Ho, ho, ho! What do you think of that?'

Poor shivering snowman! Well, he had to melt some time, hadn't he?

JACK FROST IS ABOUT

'It's cold; it's cold!' said Jean, rubbing her hands together. 'My nose is cold, my hands are cold, and so are my feet!'

'Ah, Jack Frost is about,' said her mother. 'He brings the frost and ice and snow. He's a cold fellow, is cold Jack Frost!'

'I'll go and look for him,' said Jean, and she ran out of doors. She called loudly. 'Jack Frost! Jack Frost! I don't really believe in you, but everyone talks about you, so maybe you are real after all! Jack Frost!'

'I'm here, in your snowman,' said a crackly voice. 'I'm here in the ice on the pond. I'm up on the roof in the drifts of snow there. Be careful I don't bite your nose!'

'I don't like you!' called Jean. 'You make the birds shiver. You wilt the tender plants. You bite my toes and fingers. I don't like you at all. Go away.'

'Ah, but I'm beautiful,' said Jack Frost. 'Look at the snow now – did you ever see the crystals it's made of? I make them all. Yes, and I make every one of them six-sided, but there's not two snowflakes the same!'

'I didn't know that snow crystals were so beautiful,' said Jean.

'Catch a snowflake on the arm of your coat,' cried Jack Frost. 'Are your eyes good? Then look carefully and just as it melts you'll see the beautiful six-sided crystals, all of them beautiful and all of them different!

'I'm not really cruel to the plants you know,' went on Jack Frost, his voice sounding all around her. 'They keep warm under their blanket of snow. They do, really. And when it melts, the water runs down to their roots and they drink.'

'Where are you?' said Jean, looking all about. 'Sometimes it seems it's my snowman speaking and sometimes the snow under my feet. Where are you? I don't think I do believe in you!'

'I'll come and draw on your windowpane tonight,' said Jack Frost just behind her. 'I will, I will! I'm fond of beauty, and I will draw beautiful things on your window! Which one is your bedroom?'

'That one,' said Jean, pointing. 'Well, you draw some lovely pictures there, Jack Frost, and maybe I'll believe in you!'

The windowpane was clear when Jean went to bed that night – but in the morning what a surprise! The whole of the pane was patterned in frost! Jack Frost had drawn fern fronds, and leaves and trees all over the window!

'He's real then!' said Jean. 'Mummy, look what Jack Frost has done. Just look!'

Has he ever done it to your window? Doesn't he draw beautifully?

THE SQUIRREL AND THE PIXIE

There was once a pixie called Goldie because of her shining yellow hair. All the summer she played with the swallows in the air, and when they flew away she was sad.

'The cold days are coming,' twittered the swallows to her. 'We must go. You cannot come with us, Goldie, because your wings could not fly so far. Why do you not sleep through the cold days as many of the other creatures do?'

'I think I will,' said Goldie. So she set about making herself some warm rugs and blankets, a warm dress and a warm cloak.

'Then I shall be able to sleep in comfort,' she told a spider who was watching her. 'I shall roll myself up in all these warm clothes and sleep until the spring, just as you do, Spider.'

She made her blankets of rose petals sewn neatly together. She made her rugs of the thistledown that she gathered from the thistles – it looked like a furry cover when she had finished it. She sewed herself a dress and a coat of crimson creeper leaves, and she did look nice in them.

Then she went to find a place to sleep in. She chose a nice cosy corner at the bottom of some big Michaelmas daisies. They waved their pretty daisy heads far above her.

She smiled at them. 'You will shelter me when it rains,' she said. Then she curled herself up in her new rugs and went to sleep.

But alas for poor Goldie! In a few days' time, the gardener came along and cut down all the Michaelmas daisies! They were fading, and he wanted to make the garden tidy.

He very nearly trod on Goldie. She woke up in a great fright and flew away, leaving behind her beautiful warm rugs and blankets. She saw them all put into the gardener's barrow and wheeled away to be burnt on the bonfire. She was very unhappy.

146

'I am so cold,' she shivered. 'I shall not be able to make any more covers. I shall freeze to death at night!'

A small red squirrel bounded over to her. 'Why are you crying?' he asked, and Goldie told him.

'Well, why don't you go and cuddle up to one of the little animals who sleep the winter days away?' he asked her. 'They usually have plenty of moss and dead leaves for blankets, or at any rate some sort of shelter from winter storms.'

'That's a very good idea,' said Goldie, cheering up. 'But where shall I find anybody? I don't know where to look.'

'Oh, I'll soon show you one or two,' said the squirrel. 'First of all, come and see the nice cosy hole that the hedgehog is sleeping in. He always makes himself very comfortable for the winter.'

Goldie took the squirrel's paw and he led her to a little hole in a dry bank. He pushed aside a mossy curtain and Goldie slipped inside. She saw a big brown prickly hedgehog there, fast asleep, curled up warmly on some dead leaves.

She came out of the hole again and shook her head. 'No, dear Squirrel,' she said, 'I don't want to sleep with the hedgehog. He is so prickly that I couldn't cuddle up to him – and besides, he snores! Take me somewhere else.'

'Well, I'll take you to the toad,' said the squirrel. 'He always chooses a good sheltered place.'

So he took the pixie to a big mossy stone, and told her to creep underneath it. There she found the old toad sleeping soundly, quite safe and cosy under the stone. But Goldie crept out again, shivering.

'He has no blankets to cover himself,' she said. 'And it is damp under there. I wouldn't like to sleep there.'

'Well, come where the bats live,' said the squirrel. 'They sleep very soundly indeed.' So he took her to an old cave and showed her the black bats hanging upside down around the cave. But Goldie screwed up her little nose and ran outside the cave.

'They smell,' she said. 'I couldn't possibly sleep with the bats.'

The squirrel thought for a moment. 'You might like to cuddle in a heap with the snakes,' he said. 'They have chosen a good hollow tree this winter, and they are so comfortable there. Come along. I'll show you.'

But when Goldie peeped inside the hollow tree and saw the snakes all twisted up together, she shook her head at once.

'No,' she said. 'I wouldn't dare to sleep with the snakes! See how they have twisted themselves together, Squirrel! They might squeeze me to bits if they twisted round me too! No! Show me someone else, please.'

'You are very hard to please, Goldie,' said the squirrel, thinking hard. 'There's the dormouse – he has quite a nice winter nest in the roots of the old fir tree. Would you like to go there?'

'Oh, I don't think so,' said Goldie. 'It sounds too stuffy to me. What about *you*, Squirrel? Where do *you* sleep?'

'Oh, I sleep in a hole in a tree, and am very cosy,' said the squirrel. 'But I don't sleep all the winter through, you know. I wake up when we get warm days and I go out and have a play. I eat a few of my nuts too. I hide them away so that I can have a feast in the warm winter days – we do get quite nice sunny days sometimes, you know, and I always think it's such a pity to sleep through those.'

'I agree with you!' cried Goldie joyfully. 'I'd like to wake up sometimes too, and have a feast of nuts.'

'The only thing is I often forget where I hide my nuts,' said the squirrel. 'I'd love to have you share my sleeping hole, Goldie, if you'd help me to hunt for my nuts when we wake.'

'I'll help you! I'll help you!' cried Goldie. 'Now show me

where you sleep, Squirrel.'

So he showed her his sheltered hole in the oak tree, and together they curled up there, warm and happy. Goldie cuddled right into the squirrel's lovely fur, and it was just like a cosy rug.

'I'm so happy,' she said sleepily. 'This is better than squeezing in with the snakes – or getting a cold under the toad's stone – or hanging upside down with the bats! Goodnight, dear Squirrel! Sleep tight!'

They did – and on the first warm winter days they will wake, and you may see them hunting for the nuts that the squirrel so carefully hid away. If you see him, look out for Goldie – she is very much better at finding the nuts than he is!

THE BONFIRE FOLK

Peter and Jean were running home from school one day when they passed the cobbler's shop. Mr Knock the cobbler was sitting cross-legged in his window mending somebody's shoes.

His glass window was closed for it was a cold day. Peter knocked on it, for he and Jean always liked to have a smile from the old cobbler. He had eyes as blue as forget-me-nots, and whiskers as white as snow.

Mr Knock looked up and smiled, then beckoned the children inside. They opened the door and walked in, sniffing the good smell of leather.

'Did you want us, Mr Knock?' asked Peter.

'Yes,' said Mr Knock. 'I want to know if you'll do an old man a good turn. My errand boy's ill and there are three pairs of shoes to be sent out. Do you think you and Jean could deliver them for me on your way home?'

'Of course, Mr Knock,' said Peter. 'We'd love to. Where are they?'

The old cobbler gave three parcels to them. 'That's for Captain Brown,' he said. 'That's for Mrs Lee – and that little one is for Mrs George's baby. You know where they all live, don't you?'

'Yes, Mr Knock!' said the children, pleased. It was fun to play at being errand boys! They rushed off with the parcels, and left them at the right houses. Then they went home to dinner. On their way to afternoon school they went to see Mr Knock again.

'We left all your parcels safely for you,' said Peter.

'Thank you kindly,' said Mr Knock. 'Now what would you like for a reward?'

'Nothing!' said Jean at once. 'We did it for you because we

like you. We don't want to be paid.'

'Well, I won't pay you,' said Mr Knock, his blue eyes shining. 'But I happen to know something you badly want and maybe I'll be able to help you to get it. I know that you want to see the fairy folk, don't you?'

'Oooh, yes,' said both children at once, 'but we never have.'

'Well, I'll tell you a time *I* saw them,' said Mr Knock, almost in a whisper. 'I saw them one cold winter night, my dears – all toasting themselves beside my father's bonfire at the bottom of the garden. I've never told anyone till today – but now I'm telling you, for maybe you'll see them there too!'

Well! The children were so surprised that they could hardly say a word. They went off to school full of excitement. Daddy was at home that day and meant to make a bonfire, they knew. Suppose, just suppose, they saw the little folk round the flames?

They went down to look at the bonfire after school. Daddy said he was going to put it out soon, and the children were disappointed. They ran off to some woods nearby, and, in the half dark, managed to find some dry fir cones. 'We'll use these to keep the fire in after tea,' said Jean. 'They burn beautifully.'

They placed a little pile of them beside the still burning fire, and ran in to tea – but afterwards Auntie Mollie came and the two children had to stay and talk to her. It was their bedtime before they could think of going down to the bonfire again.

'Let's creep down now and see if anyone is there,' said Jean. 'I *would* so like to see. It's very cold and frosty tonight – maybe there will be one or two of the little folk there already.'

They put on their coats, their hats and their scarves. They opened the garden door softly. They crept down the garden, walking on the grass so that their feet should make no noise.

'The bonfire is still burning,' whispered Jean. 'It didn't go out after all. Can you see anyone there?'

The children went round a hedge and came in sight of the fire. It was burning brightly, and the smoke swirled away from it, smelling delicious. Jean and Peter stopped and looked.

'There's Whiskers, our cat, sitting by it!' said Jean in a delighted whisper. 'And look – there's the cat next door too! Both warming their toes!'

'What's that the other side?' whispered back Peter. 'I think – I really do think it's a brownie!'

154

It was! He was a tiny little man with a long beard and twinkling eyes. He was throwing fir cones on the fire. No wonder it was burning brightly!

'It's the fir cones we collected!' said Jean. 'How lovely! Oh, look – here's someone coming!'

Somebody came out of the shadowy bushes and sat down by the fire. It was an elf with long shining wings. She spoke to the cats and the brownie and they all nodded to her. They knew one another, it was quite certain. The fairy had brought some bundles of small twigs with her and these she threw every now and again on the fire, making it burn even more brightly.

Then a hedgehog came, and a rabbit. They sat down by the bonfire, and the rabbit held out both his paws to the flames. Jean and Peter thought he looked lovely.

'Isn't this exciting?' whispered Jean. 'I never thought we'd see all this! Do you suppose everybody's bonfires have bonfire folk round them at night?'

'I expect so,' said Peter. 'Oh, Jean, do let's go and speak to them all! I'm sure they won't be frightened.'

The two children left the hedge they were standing by and walked softly to the bonfire. Nobody saw them at first – and

then the two cats pricked up their ears, spied them both, and shot away like shadows.

Peter caught hold of the brownie and held him tightly. 'Don't be afraid,' he said. 'I just want to speak to you. This is our bonfire and we are so pleased to see you come and warm yourselves by it. I am glad you used the fir cones to make it burn brightly.'

'Oh, did *you* leave the fir cones?' said the brownie. 'How kind of you! The fire was nearly out, but the dry cones just got it going again nicely. You're sure you don't mind us warming ourselves here? It's so very cold tonight – and these garden bonfires are so useful to us little folk.'

'You come whenever you like,' said Peter, letting go of the brownie, now that the little man knew the children were friends. For a few minutes they all sat there together, and the rabbit was just about to jump on to Jean's knee when the children heard their mother calling.

'Peter! Jean! You naughty children! Surely you haven't gone out into the cold garden! Come to bed at once.'

'Goodbye!' said the children to the bonfire folk. 'Tell everybody to use our fire each night. We like to know you are there.' And off they ran to bed.

157

They love to think of all the little bonfire-folk sitting round the smoky fire in the garden. Do *you* ever have a bonfire? Well, maybe the little folk are round yours too, warming their toes on a winter's evening! Wouldn't I love to see them!

BEDROOMS FOR THE BIRDS

'Mother, are the birds very cold at night when the frost comes?' asked Donald, looking up at the stars as he and his mother walked home from his aunt's house.

'Very cold,' said Mother. 'You see, they haven't a nice warm house with a roof and walls as you have, Donald. And they have no warm bed with blankets!'

'Where do they sleep?' said Donald. 'I can't see or hear any birds now, Mother. Where are they?'

'They find sheltered places in thick evergreen bushes, or

behind the ivy on the wall,' said Mother. 'They like the yew bushes too, because those are thick and close-growing. But many little birds get frozen at night, Donald, when it is as cold as this.'

'Oh, I wish they didn't,' said Donald. The wind blew cold around him, and the tip of his nose felt frozen. Donald felt certain that there must be many birds shivering in the wind that night.

'Mother, Tommy Green has two nesting boxes in his garden, and he says that the tits go there to sleep at night,' said Donald. 'Do you think they would be warm and cosy there?'

'Oh yes,' said Mother. 'They would be very happy. But there are not many nesting boxes in gardens, Donald. One here and there – not nearly enough for all the birds.'

'I *would* like some in our garden,' said Donald. 'Mother, will you buy twelve? That would be enough for all the birds in our garden, wouldn't it?'

'Yes, but, my dear Donald, I haven't nearly enough money to buy twelve nesting boxes!' cried Mother.

'Oh, Mother, I do, do so want to give the birds good sleeping places,' said Donald, disappointed. 'I shan't be able to go to sleep at night if I think of all the birds shivering and shaking in this frosty wind, and perhaps waking up dead tomorrow.'

'Well, darling, you needn't go to the expense of buying twelve nesting boxes!' said Mother. 'You can easily give them something else they will like just as well, and which won't cost you a penny.'

'Oh, Mother, what?' asked Donald.

'You can find small flowerpots in the shed,' said Mother. 'And you can put a little loose hay into each. And then you can find good places *in* the bushes or under them, and put the pots there. The birds will soon find them and will be delighted with them!'

'Will they sleep in them?' asked Donald.

'Of course,' said Mother. 'If you'd like to do that, I will take you round the garden one night with a torch, and you can see if any bird has taken your little bedrooms!'

Donald thought that was a wonderful idea. He could get enough bedrooms for all the birds in his garden, he was sure. He thought he would count them tomorrow morning.

So the next day he watched from the window to see how many birds came to eat the few breakfast crumbs he had scattered on the grass. He counted – one, two, three, four, five, six sparrows – three tits – two robins – one thrush – two chaffinches – goodness, what a lot of birds! He would need at least twelve flowerpots!

He set off to find them. There was a whole row of them in the shed, set neatly inside one another. Donald took twelve of the smaller ones. Then he looked about for some hay to put inside them. There was some stacked in a corner. He pulled out what he wanted.

He stuffed hay loosely into each pot. It took quite a long time. Then he set out to look for good places to put them. He was sure he knew some.

Yes, one pot could quite well be tucked inside that privet hedge. And one could be tucked under the lilac bush, and another into that thick ivy. And two could go into the yew bushes. Really, it was quite easy to find good places. Donald put each of the twelve pots somewhere, laying them on their side, so that the birds would have a roof to shelter them, and walls all round them except at the front.

'They can pull the hay in front of them for a blanket if they want to,' said Donald, pleased. 'There, they have got bedrooms

162

and blankets now, tucked into the bushes. Won't they be glad?'

He told Mother what he had done. She was pleased. 'Now we will give the birds a night or two to get used to your bedrooms,' she said, 'and then we will put on hats and coats and scarves, and go and peep at them with a torch. That will be fun!'

So two or three nights later, Mother and Donald set out with a torch. Donald took her to the ivy. She shone her torch inside the pot. No bird was there! How disappointing!

They went to the next pot. No bird was there either! Really, it was very strange. It was not until they came to the eighth pot that they found anything – and in that pot, fast asleep, with his tiny blue head tucked under his wing, was a bluetit! He did not even wake when the torch shone on him. Donald was delighted.

'Oh, isn't he sweet?' he cried. 'Oh, Mother, does he like his bedroom and blanket, do you think? Look how he has tucked the hay round himself!'

'Now I wonder why this one pot has a bird in and not the others,' said Mother. She thought for a minute and then she nodded her head. 'Yes, I think I know, Donald. This one is turned right away from the wind, which is very, very cold tonight. I believe you have put all the others so that the wind blows straight into them. Those bedrooms would be very cold indeed! Tomorrow you must turn them so that they do not face the wind.'

Only that one pot had a bird inside. Mother and Donald went indoors, and Donald made up his mind to turn all the pots the right way tomorrow.

So in the morning he very busily turned this one round and that one round. At last not one faced the cold wind. They were all turned away from it. Donald even stuffed up the little hole at the bottom of each pot with wet earth so that not the tiniest draught could get into the bedroom!

And then, when he had finished, he made a sad discovery. He had dropped his silver pencil somewhere! It was his best and favourite pencil, with his name on it. Uncle Jack had given it to him when he had come home from the war, and Donald was very proud of it because it had little Union Jacks all round it, done in red, white and blue.

'Oh, bother!' said Donald, and he began to hunt for it. He hunted and hunted – but the pencil was nowhere to be seen. It must have dropped out of his pocket when he went to turn the

164

flowerpots round. It was too bad!

'Things like that shouldn't happen when I am doing a good turn to the birds,' grumbled Donald. 'If I was being naughty, it would be a good punishment to lose my best Union Jack pencil – but I was being kind.'

'Yes, it's too bad, darling,' said Mother. 'But things often happen like that. Don't grumble about it. You may suddenly find it.'

But he didn't find it and he was very unhappy about it, for it is horrid to lose anything. Mother went to see the flowerpots and she said he had put them beautifully out of the wind. 'I shouldn't be surprised if you find every one of them full on the next frosty night,' she said.

So, when the wind blew extra cold one night, the two of them went out with a torch once more – and do you know, every single pot was full! And one pot even had two birds in! Two bluetits slept there side by side. They did look sweet. A robin slept in another pot. A hedge sparrow slept in another, and a big blackbird had squeezed himself into one too. All the rest had little brown house sparrows, who awoke as soon as the torch shone down on them, but did not try to fly away.

'Oh, Mother! I think it's lovely, don't you?' said Donald. 'All my bedrooms are full – every one of them – and did you see how the birds had pulled the hay about them, just as we pull blankets round us? I do feel happy. None of our birds will die of the cold at night, will they?'

'No,' said Mother. 'That will be a good thing – for in the springtime we need all the birds there are to eat the caterpillars and grubs and greenfly from our plants. You help the birds in winter, Donald – and they will help you in the spring!'

'Well, I wish they'd help me to find my silver pencil,' said Donald, as they went back to the house. 'Every time I think of that I feel horrid. I did love that pencil so. Do you think the birds could find it for me?'

'I shouldn't think so,' said Mother.

But she was wrong! What do you think happened the very next day? Why, Donald saw a robin turning over dead leaves in the little ditch under the hedge, and he shouted to his mother.

'Mother! Look at that robin! It's hunting for my pencil! It's turning over all the leaves to find it. Look!'

Mother looked, and she laughed. 'No,' she said. 'It is looking for tiny insects that may be hiding under the dead leaves, Donald. It won't find your pencil for you.'

'Well, I'm going to see,' said Donald, and he ran out. He went to the ditch, and the robin looked up at him with a friendly black eye. '*Tirra-lee!*' said the robin, and threw a dead leaf neatly over his shoulder.

And there, where the leaf had been, was the Union Jack pencil! Donald gave such a squeal that the robin flew off in fright. Donald picked up his pencil. The silver was dull and stained – but it was his lovely pencil all the same! Oh, how marvellous!

'Mother! Mother! The robin *was* looking for my pencil, and he's found it for me – look, look!' cried Donald, rushing indoors. 'It was under a leaf in the ditch. Oh, how glad I am that I did a good turn to the birds! I *know* that robin tried to do me a good turn back!'

'Well, perhaps he did,' said Mother, and she took the pencil to clean it and make it bright again. 'There! It is as good as new! Now you have a wonderful story to tell all your friends, Donald – how you gave the birds bedrooms in your garden – and how the robin hunted for and found your silver pencil!'

You can give *your* garden birds some bedrooms and blankets too. You *will* like seeing them cuddled up fast asleep, with their tiny heads under their wings!

THE WINTER WIDE-AWAKES

Mother put her head in at the nursery door and saw a very cosy scene. There was a big fire burning, and three children were sitting by it. Two were playing a game of snap, and the other was reading.

'Do you know who's here?' she said. 'Auntie Lou.'

'Oh!' said all three children, raising their heads. They were Tessie, Pat and Johnny. Tessie looked a little doubtful.

'I hope she hasn't come to take us for a walk,' she said. 'Auntie Lou is lovely to go for walks with in the summer, but it's all snowy outside now and very cold. I don't think I want to go out today.'

Another head came round the door. It belonged to Auntie Lou. She was dressed in warm tweeds, and had a bright red scarf round her neck. Her head was bare, and her cheeks were as red as her scarf. Her blue eyes twinkled.

'What's this I hear? You don't want to go out with me? Well, I like that! Who came and begged to go out with me every week in the summer? Who went to find conkers and nuts and blackberries with me in the autumn because I knew all the best places?'

'We did,' said Pat with a grin. 'But, Auntie Lou, we're so warm and cosy here, and there's nothing to see in the country now. Honestly there isn't.'

'There's nothing but snow,' said Johnny, 'and all the birds are gone, and all the animals are asleep.'

'What a poor little ignorant boy!' said Auntie Lou, making a funny face. 'It's true we shouldn't see anything of the winter sleepers – they're all tucked away in their holes – but we could see plenty of wide-awakes.'

'Who are they?' asked Johnny.

170.

'Well, as I came over the fields this morning to pay a call on three lazy children, I saw a beautiful red fox,' said Auntie Lou. 'He wasn't asleep. He almost bumped into me coming round the hedge. I didn't hear him and I suppose he didn't hear me.'

'Oh, a fox!' said Pat. 'I'd like to have seen that. Auntie, I'll come with you if you'll show me all the wide-awakes.'

'We'll all come,' said Tessie, shutting her book. 'I'd like to find some wide-awakes too, and some birds as well. Lots have gone away, but we've still plenty left, haven't we, Auntie?'

'Plenty,' said her aunt. 'Hurry up then. I'll give you three minutes to put on boots and coats.'

They were all ready quickly, for they knew perfectly well that Auntie Lou wouldn't wait for anyone who wasn't. They set off down the snowy garden path.

'You can see how many birds have been in your garden this morning,' said Auntie Lou, pointing to some bird tracks in the snow. 'Look, that's where the sparrows have been. See the little footmarks all set out in pairs? That's because they hop with their feet together. And there are the marks of a running bird – his footmarks are behind one another.'

Johnny hopped with his feet together, and then ran. He saw that he had left his first footmarks in pairs, but the other marks were spread out behind one another. Auntie Lou laughed. 'The footmarks of the Johnny-Bird,' she said.

By the frozen pond they came to other bird prints, and Tessie pointed to them. 'Ducks,' she said. 'You can see the marks of the webbing between their toes.'

'Yes. The poor things thought they might have a swim on the pond, and came waddling up from the farm to see,' said Auntie Lou. 'I wonder what they think when they find they can't splash in the ice.'

They left the pond behind and struck across the fields. How lovely they were, all blanketed in snow! The hedges were sprinkled with snow too, but here and there the red hips showed the green unripe ivy berries.

'Look, Auntie,' said Pat, pointing to some bark in the hedgerow that had been gnawed white. 'Who's been doing that? Somebody must have been very hungry to eat bark.'

'One of the most wide-awakes,' said Auntie Lou. She pointed to some tracks. 'Look, rabbit footmarks. The bunnies have been gnawing bark because they are so hungry.'

172

'But why don't they eat the grass?' said Tessie.

The two boys laughed at her. 'How can they when it's deep down under the snow?' said Pat scornfully. 'Use your brains, Tessie!'

'Oh, I never thought of that,' said Tessie. 'Poor little rabbits – they must get awfully hungry when their grass is hidden away. No wonder they come and gnaw at the bark.'

'Yes, and the fox knows they will come out to feed somewhere,' said Auntie Lou. 'So he comes out too, and pads along quietly in the snow, watching for an unwary rabbit. I saw a sad little scattering of grey fur this morning as I came along, to show me where the fox had made his breakfast.'

'Look, what's that?' suddenly whispered Johnny, clutching at his aunt's arm. She looked where he was pointing.

'A stoat,' she said. 'He's after the rabbits, I expect.'

'But he's white,' said Johnny, amazed. 'He wasn't white when we saw him in the summer.'

'Ah, he's clever. He changed his dark coat for a white one in the winter when the snow came,' said his aunt, 'all but the tip of his tail, which is black. Now his enemies can't see him against the white snow.'

'Isn't he clever?' said Pat. 'He's cleverer than the fox. *He* doesn't change his red coat to white. Does the stoat always change his coat, Auntie Lou?'

'Only in cold climates,' said his aunt, 'not down in the south where it is warmer and there is little snow in the winter. Now look, what's that?'

'A weasel,' said Pat. 'He's wide awake too, isn't he? Look at him, going along almost like a slinky snake. He's a fierce, lively little fellow.'

They went by another farm. The farmer was standing at the door of his cow shed and hailed them.

'Good morning. It's a fine morning for a walk, isn't it? It's a pity I can't send my cows out for a walk too. They're tired of standing in their sheds.'

'Farmer Toms, have you lots of mice and rats about?' asked Johnny. 'We're out looking for wide-awake creatures today, and we've seen plenty, but we've seen no rats nor mice.'

'Ah, I've too many – far too many,' said the farmer. 'Up in the loft there, where I store my grain, I get no end of the creatures. You go up and maybe you'll see some.'

They all climbed the ladder and went into the dark loft. They sat down on sacks and kept quiet. Almost at once they heard a squeaking. Then two mice appeared from a hole and scampered over to a bin.

'There are two,' called Tessie, but her voice frightened them of course, and they turned to run away, then a rat suddenly appeared and made a dart at one of the mice.

Tessie gave a squeal.

'Oh! A rat! Horrid, sharp-nosed thing! Auntie, I don't like rats. Let's go down.'

The mice disappeared, and the rat slunk away too. He was a thin rat and looked very hungry. Perhaps he wasn't very clever at catching mice. Nobody liked the look of him.

'The rat is every animal's enemy, and ours as well,' said Auntie Lou. 'I haven't anything good to say of him.'

The mice squealed behind the boards. 'They are saying "Hear, hear",' said Pat, and that made everyone laugh.

They went down the ladder, and told Farmer Toms what they had seen. Then they went into the shed. The cows smelt nice, and turned their big heads to look at the children.

'Where are your sheep?' asked Johnny.

The farmer waved his hand up to the hills. 'Away up there in

176

the snow with the shepherd,' he said. 'He's got them safe, and is expecting their little lambs soon. They're often born in the snowy weather, and they're none the worse for it. You must go and see them when they are born.'

The children left the farm and went on their way.

'I wouldn't have believed there was so much to see on a snowy wintry day,' said Tessie. 'I really wouldn't. Why, it's as interesting as summertime.'

'Look, there's a thrush – and a blackbird too – eating the hips in the snowy hedge,' said Pat. 'Aren't they enjoying themselves? What a good thing there are berries to feed the hungry birds in the winter!'

'And look at all those chaffinches,' said Tessie, as a flock of the bright little birds flew over her head towards the farm. 'I've never seen so many chaffinches together before.'

'No, in the spring and summer they go about in pairs,' said her aunt. 'But many birds in winter like to flock together. They are probably going to see if there is any grain round about the farm for them to peck up. Look up into the sky – you'll see some other birds there that flock by the thousand.'

'Peewits!' said Johnny. 'Don't their wings twinkle as they fly?

I do love their call too – just like their name!'

'I should think we've seen all the winter wide-awakes there are now,' said Tessie. But Auntie Lou shook her head.

'No, there's another. I saw him this morning as I came through the hazel wood. He *has* been asleep, but this lovely sunny day woke him up. He doesn't mind the snow a bit. Look, there he is, the pretty thing!'

A squirrel suddenly bounded down a tree trunk and ran right over to the children. Auntie Lou put her hand in her pocket and took out a few shelled nuts. 'Here you are,' she said to the amusing little squirrel. 'I've shelled them for you, so you won't have any bother today.'

The squirrel took a nut from her fingers, skipped away a few paces, and then sat up with the nut in his paws and began to eat it quickly. The children watched him in delight.

'He's a great friend of mine,' said Auntie Lou. 'If he's awake and I walk through his wood, he always comes along to me to see if I've anything for him. I expect he has plenty of nuts and acorns hidden away, but he does love a peanut or Brazil nut all ready shelled for him – it makes a change from his own nuts.'

'Let's take him home! Oh, do let's take him home!' said

178

Johnny, and he tried to catch the bush-tailed squirrel; but in a trice the little creature ran up a nearby trunk, his tail out behind him, and sat high above their heads, making a little chattering noise.

'His home is up in that tree,' said Auntie Lou. 'I've no doubt he has a very cosy hole there, safe from little boys who want to take him home with them.'

'Oh, I do like him,' said Johnny. 'Perhaps in the spring, when he has tiny young squirrel children I could have one of those. I'd love a squirrel pet. I'd call him Scamper.'

The squirrel disappeared into his home. Auntie Lou began to walk through the trees. 'It's time we went home too,' she said. 'Look how the sun is sinking. It will soon be getting dark. Come along.'

They ran after her, looking about for more squirrels, but they saw none. Johnny made up his mind to go to the woods the very next day and make friends with the little squirrel all by himself.

'He's the nicest winter wide-awake we've seen,' he said. 'What a lot we've met today, Auntie! I'd no idea there were so many birds and animals to see on such a wintry day.'

It began to get dark. 'We shan't see any more now,' said

Tessie. But they did! As they walked down the lane home, a little bird kept pace with them, flying from tree to tree as they went, giving them little bursts of song.

'It's a robin,' said Auntie Lou. 'He is always the latest bird abed. Maybe he's the one that belongs to your garden, children. Look out for him tomorrow, and scatter some crumbs for him.'

'We will,' said Tessie, opening the garden gate. The robin flew in before her. 'Yes, he must be ours. He has come to welcome us home. Auntie, you're coming in to tea, aren't you?'

'Of course,' said Auntie Lou. 'I think I deserve a very nice tea, with hot scones and homemade jam, after taking you three children out to see so many wide-awakes.'

'You do! You do!' chorused the children. And she did, didn't she? I hope you'll see a lot of wide-awakes if *you* go out on a winter's day.

WANTED — A ROYAL SNOW-DIGGER

Once upon a time the fairy queen wanted a royal snow-digger, who would dig away the snow from her palace gates after a snowstorm. So she sent out Domino the brownie and told him to find somebody. Off he went, the feather in his cap waving merrily. He was sure that anyone would be pleased to be made Royal Snow-Digger to Her Majesty the Queen.

First he went to Slicker the grass snake, who lay basking in the sunshine of the pretty autumn day.

'Slicker,' he said, 'will you be Royal Snow-Digger to the queen, and dig away the snow from the palace gates after a snowstorm?'

'What is snow?' asked Slicker in wonder. 'I have never seen it. I sleep all the winter through, Domino, in the hollow tree over there, curled up with my brothers and sisters. I cannot be Royal Snow-Digger.'

Domino ran off, disappointed. He went to the cornfield where Dozy the little dormouse used to live – but Dozy had run from the field when the corn was cut and was now in the hazel copse, hunting for fallen nuts. Domino found him there, as fat as butter.

'Dozy,' he said, 'will you be Royal Snow-Digger to the queen and dig away the snow from the palace gates after a snowstorm?'

'Not I!' said Dozy, rubbing his fat little sides. 'I shall sleep all the winter through. See how fat I am! I shall not need any food all the cold-weather time. It is stupid to wake up when it is cold. Far better to sleep. I shall be hidden in a warm bank down in a cosy hole, Domino, when the snow comes. I don't want to dig snow for the queen.'

Domino ran off, quite cross with the fat little dormouse. He came to where the swallows flew high in the air, and called to them, for he knew that the fairy queen was fond of the steel-blue birds.

'Swallows,' he called, 'will you be Royal Snow-Digger to the queen and dig away the snow from the palace gates after a snowstorm?'

'Twitter, twitter, Domino!' called the swallows, laughing. 'Why, we shall not be here much longer! We never wait for snow and frost. It is too cold for us in the wintertime here, and besides there are no flies to eat. No, no, we are going to fly away south, far away to the warm countries where nobody has ever seen such a strange thing as snow.'

Domino sighed. He would never find a snow-digger for the queen. It was strange. He wondered who to ask next.

I'll ask the big badger, he thought. *He would make a fine snow-digger, for he has great paws, strong and sturdy.*

So he went to where the badger was walking on the hillside and called to him.

'Hey, Brock the badger!' he cried. 'Will you be Royal Snow-Digger to the queen and dig away the snow from the palace gates after a snowstorm?'

'I should like to very much,' said Brock. 'But, you know, Domino, I cannot keep awake in the wintertime. I simply have to go to sleep. I am lining a nice big hole in the hillside now, with all sorts of warm things – dead leaves and bracken and big cushions of moss – to make me and my family a warm bed for the winter. We always sleep through the cold weather.'

'Dear, dear, what lazy creatures you must be!' said Domino crossly. 'Well, I'll go and find someone else. They can't all be as lazy as you, Brock!'

Soon Domino met the hedgehog, Spiny, and he waved his hand to him brightly.

'Hey, Spiny!' he called. 'Wait a minute! I want to ask you something. Will you be Royal Snow-Digger to the queen and dig away the snow from the palace gates after a snowstorm?'

'I'd like to, Domino,' said Spiny, shuffling in the dead leaves. 'But, you know, I hide away in the ditch all winter through. I can't bear the cold weather. You won't find me after a snowstorm! No, I cannot be Royal Snow-Digger. But look — there goes Crawler the toad. Ask him.'

The toad was crawling on the damp side of the ditch, so Domino jumped across and spoke to him.

'Crawler, will you be Royal Snow-Digger to the queen and dig away the snow from the palace gates after a snowstorm?' he asked.

'No,' said Crawler, blinking his lovely coppery eyes, 'I won't. I am a sensible person and I like to sleep under a damp stone when frost and snow are about. It's no use asking my cousins the frogs, either — they sleep upside down in the pond, tucked comfortably away in the mud at the bottom. Goodbye!'

'There aren't many more people to ask,' said Domino to

himself. 'Dear, dear me – I can't possibly go home to the queen and tell her that I can find nobody. She would make me Royal Snow-Digger and that's a job I should hate! Too much hard work about it for me! Hello, there goes Bushy the squirrel. He's a lively chap. He'd make a splendid snow-digger.'

So he called to Bushy the squirrel, who was hiding nuts away in a hollow tree.

'Bushy! Bushy! Will you be Royal Snow-Digger and sweep away the snow from the palace gates after a snowstorm?' he called. 'You don't sleep all the winter, do you?'

'Well, not exactly,' said the squirrel. 'But I only wake up on nice sunny days, Domino. I sleep curled up in my tail in a hollow tree when it's really cold. I'm not sure I would wake up after a snowstorm. In fact, I'm quite sure I couldn't. But you can try to wake me if you like.'

'Oh no, thanks,' said Domino in disgust. 'I must have someone I can trust to be on the spot. I don't want to go hunting in all the hollow trees in the wood to find you on a snowy day!'

He turned away and went back towards the palace. As he went he heard a little voice calling him. He looked round. It was Bobtail the sandy rabbit.

'I heard what you were asking Bushy the squirrel,' said Bobtail. 'Do you think I would do for Royal Snow-Digger, Domino? I'd love to try.'

'Oh, I expect you sleep all the winter, don't you, like the others?' said Domino gloomily. 'Or you stand on your head in the pond? Or line a hole in a bank and snore there? I don't believe there's any use in asking you to be Royal Snow-Digger.'

'Oh, Domino, I keep awake all the winter!' said Bobtail. 'Yes, I do, really. I'm used to the snow. And there is my cousin the hare, too – he's out all the winter. And so are the weasels and the stoats – but don't let's talk of them! They are cruel fellows, and no gentlemen!'

'Well, you can be Royal Snow-Digger then,' said Domino. 'Come along to the queen and she will give you your snow-digger badge. But mind, Bobtail, if you suddenly make up your mind to do what nearly all the others do – sleep, or fly away, or hide somewhere – I'll hunt you out and pull your tail.'

'I shan't do any of those things,' said Bobtail happily. He walked to the palace with Domino the brownie, and the queen hung a little golden badge round his neck: on it was printed ROYAL SNOW-DIGGER.

And now every winter the rabbits are the Queen's snow-diggers. They sweep away the snow from the palace gates after a snowstorm, and never dream of going to sleep like the toads and hedgehogs, the badgers and the squirrels.

If you see a rabbit out in the snow, look at him carefully. If he has a golden badge hung round his neck, you'll know what he is – a royal snow-digger!

SANTA'S WORKSHOP

In the nursery all the toys were getting ready for Christmas. The doll's house dolls were making paper chains and the wind-up sailor was baking mince pies. Even Panda was helping to make decorations, and he had only arrived in the nursery three weeks before – a present from the children's Aunt Jane.

All the toys were helping, except for one – the big rocking horse that lived in the middle of the nursery floor. He was a fine fellow with a lovely spotted coat, a big mane and a bushy black tail.

He rocked back and forth and took the children for long rides around the nursery floor. They loved him – but the toys were afraid of him.

Sometimes he would begin to rock when they were playing around, and then, how they ran out of the way! Sometimes he was so proud and so vain that he would not play with the other nursery toys.

'I'm too important to do boring things like making paper chains,' he boasted. 'I'm the only toy in this nursery big enough for the children to ride on. I ought to be king of the nursery for Christmas.'

'Well, you don't deserve to be,' said the curly-haired doll. 'You squashed the monkey's tail yesterday, and that was unkind.'

'I didn't mean to,' said the horse, offended. 'He shouldn't have left it lying around under my rockers. Silly of him.'

'You should have looked down before you began to rock, and you would have seen it,' said the doll.

'Well! Do you suppose I'm going to bother to look for tails and things before I begin to rock?' said the horse. 'You just look out for yourselves! That's the best thing to do.'

But the toys were careless. Later that morning the little red toy car ran under the horse's rockers and had his paint badly scratched. Next, the wind-up sailor left his key there and the rocking horse bent it when he rocked on it. It was difficult to wind up the sailor after that, and he was cross.

Then the curly-haired doll dropped her bead necklace and the rocking horse rocked on it and smashed some of the beads. The toys were really upset with him about that.

'Be careful, be careful!' they cried. 'Tell us before you rock, Rocking Horse! You might rock on one of us and hurt us badly!'

But the rocking horse just laughed and thought it was a great joke to scare the toys so much.

'You are not kind,' said Ben the big teddy bear. 'One day you will be sorry.'

And so he was, as you will hear.

It happened that, on the day before Christmas, Sarah and Jack had been playing with their toys and had left them all around the nursery when they had gone for lunch.

Now, the panda's head and one of his ears were just under the rocker of the rocking horse. And as soon as the children had left the room, the rocking horse decided to rock.

'Stop! Stop!' shrieked the toys, running forward. 'Panda is underneath!'

But the rocking horse didn't listen. No, he thought the toys were scared as usual, and he didn't listen to what they said. Back and forth he rocked – and poor Panda was underneath!

Oh dear, oh dear, when the toys got to him what a sight he was! Some of his nice black fur had come out, and his right ear was all squashed. The toys pulled him away and he began to cry.

'What's the matter?' asked the rocking horse, stopping and looking down.

'You naughty horse! We told you to stop! Now see what you have done!' cried the toys angrily. 'You are really very unkind. We won't speak to you or play with you any more.'

'Don't then,' said the horse, and he rocked away by himself. *Cree-eek, cree-eek!* 'I'm sure I don't want to talk to you or give you rides if you are going to be so cross with me.'

After that the toys paid no attention to the naughty rocking horse. They made a great fuss over Panda, who soon stopped crying. Then they went on getting ready for Christmas. Ben wrapped up a present for the pink cat, Curly-Haired Doll made a Christmas stocking, and Jack-in-the-Box helped the other toys hang tinsel on the Christmas tree. They had such fun!

In the corner of the nursery, Rocking Horse felt sad. He usually helped hang the tinsel because he could reach higher than the other toys.

I wish they'd talk to me! he thought to himself. *I wish they'd play. I'd like to give them each a ride around the nursery – in fact, I'd take three of them at once if they asked me.*

But the toys acted as if the rocking horse wasn't there at all. They didn't ask him to help with anything. They didn't even look at him.

'He's unkind and selfish and horrid,' they said. 'And the best way to treat people like that is not to pay any attention to them.'

So the rocking horse got sadder and sadder, and longed to gallop around the nursery just for a change. But he was afraid the toys might be cross if he did.

Now, just as it was getting dark, the children's puppy came into the nursery, because someone had left the door open. The toys fled to the toy cupboard in fear, because the puppy was very playful and liked to carry a toy outdoors and chew it.

Everyone got safely into the cupboard except the pink cat. She slipped and fell, and the puppy pounced on her. He chewed and nibbled her whiskers clean away! Nobody dared to rescue her, not even the rocking horse, though he did wonder if he should gallop at the puppy.

Then somebody whistled from downstairs, and the puppy flew out of the door.

The poor pink cat sat up. 'Oh!' she said. 'Whatever has happened to my fine pink whiskers?'

'They've gone,' said Panda, peeping out of the cupboard. 'The puppy has chewed them off. There they are, look, on the floor, in tiny little bits.'

The pink cat cried bitterly. She had been proud of her whiskers. 'A cat doesn't look like a cat without her whiskers,' she wept.

The sound of the pink cat crying made Panda feel so sad that soon he was crying too. 'What shall we do?' he wailed. 'Oh, what shall we do? When Sarah and Jack see us, all nibbled and squashed, they will throw us into the dustbin. Boo-hoo-hoo!'

'Yes,' sobbed the pink cat. 'They won't want us if they are given brand-new toys for Christmas.' And before long the nursery was filled with the sound of toys crying.

How the rocking horse wished he had not been so unkind!

He would miss any of the toys terribly if they were thrown away – and it would be mostly his fault too! Whatever could he do to earn their forgiveness? He looked around the nursery at all the Christmas decorations and suddenly he knew just what to do.

'Excuse me, toys – but I've got an idea,' he said in his humblest voice.

'It's only the rocking horse,' said Ben. 'Don't pay any attention to him.'

'Please do pay some attention,' said the horse. 'I've got a good idea. I can take all the broken toys to Santa Claus's workshop. I know the way because I came from there. Perhaps Santa Claus can fix you all and make you better.'

'But it's Christmas Eve!' cried Panda. 'Santa will be too busy delivering presents to have time for us.'

'Oh no!' replied Rocking Horse. 'Santa is the friend of every old toy. No matter how busy he is, I'm sure he will find time to help us if we ask him tonight!'

'Well! Let's go then,' said the teddy bear. So the toys helped Pink Cat and Panda, Wind-Up Sailor and the monkey, Curly-Haired Doll and the little red toy car all up on to Rocking Horse's back.

Then Ben sat at the very front and said, 'Let's go!'

Cree-eek, cree-eek! went Rocking Horse across the nursery floor and up, away out of the window and into the night sky. For miles and miles they travelled, rocking past twinkling stars towards the great hill where Santa Claus lived.

Luckily for the toys Santa was at home. He was busy piling a new load of presents on to his magic sleigh. His faithful reindeer would take them fast and far – to the other side of the world in the blink of an eye. When he heard the sound of the rocking horse neighing and *hrrumphing* at the door, he came to see who was there.

Rocking Horse explained why they had come and, to the toys' delight, Santa said he would be glad to help. He only had three more loads to deliver before morning. Then he inspected each of the toys in turn to see what the damage was.

'Dear, dear!' said Santa Claus, looking severely at the rocking horse. 'I hope you are ashamed of yourself. I have heard of you and your stupid ways of scaring the toys by rocking suddenly when they are near. Come in!'

The horse rocked in and followed Santa Claus to his workshop. In no time at all Santa had straightened out Wind-Up Sailor's

196

key and mended the curly-haired doll's broken beads. He soon fixed the monkey's squashed tail and patched up the toy car's scratched paint.

Then it was Panda's turn. Santa opened a drawer and looked into it. 'Dear me!' he said. 'I've no panda fur left. It's all been used up. Now what am I to do?'

He turned and looked at the rocking horse. 'You've a nice thick black mane!' he said. 'I think you'll have to spare a little for Panda!'

Then, to the rocking horse's horror, he took out a pair of scissors and cut a patch out of his thick mane! How strange it looked!

Quickly and neatly, Santa Claus put the black fur on to the panda's head. He stuck it there with glue, and it soon dried. Then Santa looked at Panda's squashed ear.

He found a new ear and carefully put it on. It belonged to a teddy bear, really, so it was brown, instead of black, and looked rather odd. 'Now I've no special black paint!' said Santa in a vexed tone. 'Only blue or red. That won't do for a panda's ear. Ha, I'll have to take off one of your nice black spots, Rocking Horse, and use it for the panda's ear. That will do nicely!'

198

He carefully scraped off a large spot on the horse's back, mixed it with a tiny drop of water and then painted it on Panda's new ear. It looked fine!

'Thank you very much indeed!' said the panda gratefully. 'You are very kind.'

'Not at all!' said Santa, beaming all over his big kind face. 'I'm always ready to help toys, you know! And how can I help you?' he said, looking at the pink cat.

She soon explained all about her whiskers.

'Oh dear, oh dear, oh dear!' said Santa, shaking his head sadly. 'I'm right out of whiskers.'

Just then, a small voice piped up behind him. It was Rocking Horse. 'I should be very pleased to give the toy cat some of the hairs out of my long black tail,' he said. 'They would do beautifully for whiskers.'

'But how can we get them out?' said the pink cat.

'Pull them out, of course,' said the horse.

'But it will hurt you,' said the pink cat.

'I don't mind,' said the horse bravely. 'Pull as many as you like!'

So Santa pulled eight out, and they did hurt. But the horse

didn't make a sound. Then Santa carefully gave the cat her whiskers back. 'One whisker!' he said. 'Two whiskers! Three whiskers! Oh, you will look fine when I have finished, Pink Cat. These are black whiskers, long and strong, and you will look very handsome now.' And so she did. Very fine indeed!

At last it was time to go, so all the toys clambered back on to the rocking horse.

'Thank you, Santa,' they cried as they left. 'Thank you for helping us all.'

Then off they went home again, rocking hard all the way in order to get home by morning, and glad to be good as new again. The toys cheered when they saw them.

'What glorious fur you have – and look at your fine new ear!' they cried when they saw Panda. 'And look at your lovely whiskers,' they said to Pink Cat.

Rocking Horse said nothing. He stood in the middle of the nursery floor, quite still, not a rock left in him.

'Santa took some of Rocking Horse's hair for me, and one of his spots to paint my ear black,' said Panda. 'You can see where he has a bare place on his mane, and one of his biggest spots is missing.' Sure enough, it was just as Panda had said.

200

'I must say it was nice of the rocking horse to give you them,' said Ben suddenly.

'And to give me my new whiskers,' added Pink Cat. 'Especially as we haven't even spoken to him lately. Very nice of him.'

All the other toys thought the same. So they went over to the rocking horse, who was still looking sad.

'Thank you for taking us to Santa's workshop,' said the curly-haired doll.

'It was very kind of you,' said the monkey.

'I can't thank you enough!' said the pink cat. 'I had pink whiskers before, and they didn't show up very well, but these show beautifully. Don't you think so?'

'You look very handsome,' said the horse. 'Very!'

'Your tail looks a bit thin now, I'm afraid,' said the pink cat. 'Do you mind?'

'Not a bit,' said the rocking horse. 'I can rock back and forth just as fast when my tail is thin as when it's thick. You get on my back and see, Pink Cat!'

So up got the pink cat, and the rocking horse went rocking around the nursery at top speed. It was very exciting. You may be sure the horse looked where he was going this time! He wasn't going to rock over anyone's tail again!

'Oh, thank you!' said the pink cat, quite out of breath. 'That was the nicest ride I ever had!'

'Anyone can have one!' said the horse rather gruffly, because he was afraid that the toys might say 'No', and turn their backs on him. But they didn't. They all climbed up at once.

'Nice old horse!' they said. 'We're friends again now, aren't we? Gallop away, gallop away!'

And you should have seen him gallop away again, around and around the nursery until the sun peeped through the curtains.

'Merry Christmas, Merry Christmas,' they heard the children shouting.

'Good gracious,' said Ben the teddy bear. 'It's Christmas Day!'

All the toys had quite forgotten. And a lovely Christmas Day it turned out to be too. Sarah and Jack were amazed at how smart all their old toys looked – apart from Rocking Horse, whose mane and tail looked a bit straggly.

'Never mind,' said Sarah. 'We will always love you, toys, even if you are old and worn, won't we, Jack?'

'Oh, yes,' said Jack. 'Merry Christmas, toys. Merry Christmas to you all!'

ACKNOWLEDGEMENTS

All efforts have been made to seek necessary permissions. The stories in this treasury first appeared in the following publications:

'The Thrush and His Anvil' first appeared in *Enid Blyton's Good Morning Book*, 1949.

'Gillian and the Lamb' first appeared in *Tales of Old Thatch*, 1938.

'A Little Bit of Magic' first appeared in *Sunny Stories*, No. 84, 1938.

'Confetti and Bells' first appeared as 'The Wedding of the Sailor Doll' in *Sunday Graphic*, No. 1779, 1949.

'How Very Surprising!' first appeared in *Enid Blyton's Magazine*, No. 6, Vol. 4, 1956.

'The Easter Chickens' first appeared in *Sunny Stories*, No. 66, 1938.

'The Blackbirds' Secret' first appeared as 'The Blackbird's Secret' in *Teachers World*, No. 1652, Vol. 52, 1935.

'The Great Big Shell' first appeared in *Enid Blyton's Magazine*, No. 12, Vol. 1, 1953.

'The Little Fawn' first appeared in *Teachers World*, No. 1676, Vol. 53, 1935.

ACKNOWLEDGEMENTS

'Pockets in his Knees' first appeared in *Enid Blyton's Sunny Stories*, No. 435, 1948.

'Busy-One, Help Me!' first appeared in *Enid Blyton's Magazine*, No. 17, Vol. 2, 1954.

'The Cross Old Man' first appeared in *Good Housekeeping*, No. 2, Vol. 54, 1948.

'The Three Sailors' first appeared in *Sunny Stories*, No. 82, 1938.

'The Boy Who Wouldn't Bathe' first appeared in *Teachers World*, No. 1783, Vol. 57, 1937.

'A Basket of Acorns' first appeared in *Two Years in the Infant School*, 1938.

'The Tale of Snips' first appeared in *Teachers World*, No. 1635, Vol. 51, 1934.

'Hot Potatoes' first appeared as 'Hot Potatoes!' in *Good Housekeeping*, No. 5, Vol. 52, 1947.

'The Lovely Present' first appeared in *Teachers World*, No. 1643, Vol. 52, 1934.

'Blackberry Pie' first appeared in *Teachers World*, No. 1894, Vol. 61, 1939.

'The Little Toy Maker' first appeared in *Sunny Stories*, No. 239, 1941.

'Grandpa's Conker Tree' first appeared in *Sunday Mail*, No. 1885, 1944.

'The Shivery Snowman' first appeared in *Sunny Stories for Little Folks*, No. 238, 1936.

'Jack Frost is About' first appeared as 'Jack Frost' in *Teachers World*, No. 1798, Vol. 58, 1937.

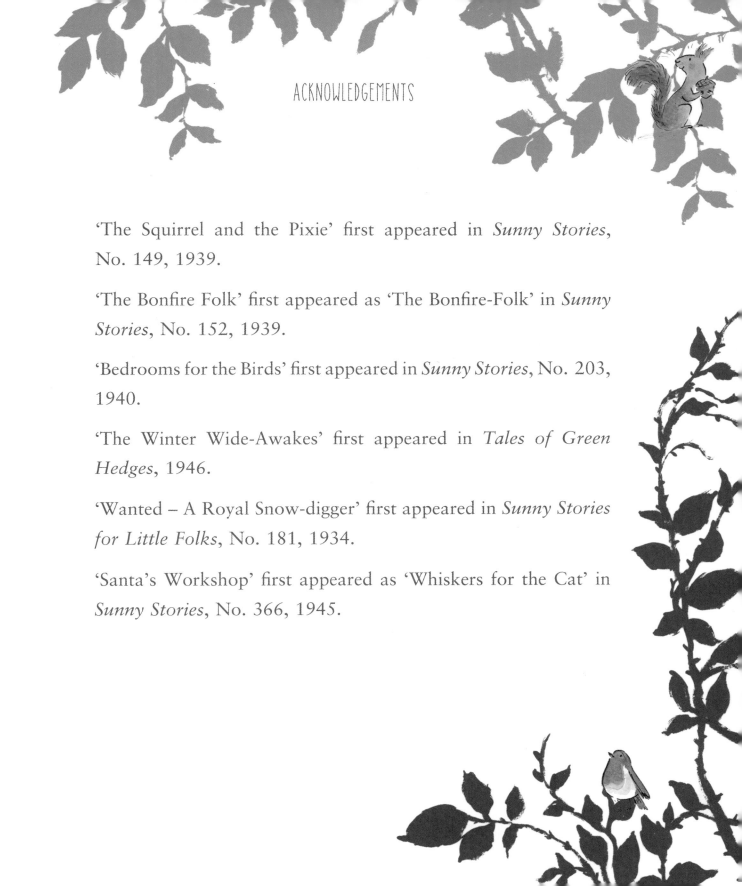

ACKNOWLEDGEMENTS

'The Squirrel and the Pixie' first appeared in *Sunny Stories*, No. 149, 1939.

'The Bonfire Folk' first appeared as 'The Bonfire-Folk' in *Sunny Stories*, No. 152, 1939.

'Bedrooms for the Birds' first appeared in *Sunny Stories*, No. 203, 1940.

'The Winter Wide-Awakes' first appeared in *Tales of Green Hedges*, 1946.

'Wanted – A Royal Snow-digger' first appeared in *Sunny Stories for Little Folks*, No. 181, 1934.

'Santa's Workshop' first appeared as 'Whiskers for the Cat' in *Sunny Stories*, No. 366, 1945.

Enid Blyton is one of the most popular children's authors of all time. Her books have sold over 500 million copies and have been translated into other languages more often than any other children's author.

Enid Blyton adored writing for children. She wrote over 700 books and about 2,000 short stories. *The Famous Five* books, now 75 years old, are her most popular. She is also the author of other favourites including *The Secret Seven*, *The Magic Faraway Tree*, *Malory Towers* and *Noddy*.

Born in London in 1897, Enid lived much of her life in Buckinghamshire and loved dogs, gardening and the countryside. She was very knowledgeable about trees, flowers, birds and animals. Dorset – where some of the Famous Five's adventures are set – was a favourite place of hers too.

Enid Blyton's stories are read and loved by millions of children (and grown-ups) all over the world. Visit enidblyton.co.uk to discover more.